CHICAGO BLOOD

DETECTIVE SHANNON ROURKE – BOOK 1

STEWART MATTHEWS

Printed in the United States of America
First Printing, 2016

Chicago Blood is a work of fiction. All aspects of the story, including
(but not limited to) incidents, dialogue, settings and characters are
creations of the author's imagination. Any similarities to any person,
living or dead, or any event, past, present or future, is coincidental.

Edited by Perry Constantine
Cover by Shayne Rutherford - www.darkmoongraphics.com
Interior Design by Colleen Sheehan - www.wdrbookdesign.com

CHAPTER 1

Everything was sideways.

All of Chicago twisted around Colm Keane when he wasn't looking. When he blinked, the sky shifted. When he tied his shoes, the traffic lights bent. When he stared into the bottom of a glass, the skyscrapers braided together.

For almost all his life, Colm closed his eyes to it. Things weren't as messed up as he thought they were—it was all in his head.

But over the last decade, the lie had unraveled.

Now his eyes were open to the only two choices he ever had. He could stay, get tangled up in all his dad's mess until he couldn't breathe anymore; or, he could go start over in Canada.

If Colm had screwed up one life, what were the odds he'd screw up a second?

He'd already stolen his ticket out of Chicago. All it took was a pregnant girlfriend with too many ideas and a pile of money big enough to buy them both a new life in Canada.

The car was packed, a couple goodbyes were said, the money was hidden, and plans were set. They'd hit the border tomorrow afternoon.

But tonight, he had one more goodbye to make.

Colm listened to the fluorescent lights hum from the ceiling. AOK King Liquor's die-cut steel shelves begged him to sip every bottle they had. The smell of mildew crept out from under the store's cracked laminate tiles, like the whole operation wanted him to grab his booze and get the hell out.

He knew he betrayed himself by being here.

But you know what, man? Forget addictions, forget troubles, forget the past—he'd earned this. For one night, he'd get to live the lie again.

One night. That's it. What was the harm in that?

Colm snatched the pint of Old Smuggler off the bottom shelf.

He knew it was cheap. It was necessary for the kind of celebration he knew he shouldn't have. Maybe he should grab the Blue Label off the top shelf—or what was that stuff in the tin? The stuff his dad liked?

Naw, forget it. If Colm was going to break his own rules, he was going to do it his way. He had good memories of Old Smuggler.

The immigrant behind the counter started at Colm as he made his way up. The guy had bug eyes and a gaunt face. His white button-up yellowed around the collar. The shirt hung over his bony shoulders like a funeral shroud at a wake.

"I ain't gonna steal nothing," Colm said.

The cashier smiled at him. One of his front teeth reached out over his bottom lip.

"You speak English?" Colm put the pint of Old Smuggler on the counter.

"No English," the cashier said. He had a thick accent. Something African.

Colm didn't know about Africa. He'd seen that *Hotel Rwanda* movie once. It had been crazy enough to put him off learning anything else about that place, not that he had the time.

"Eleven dollars, one cent," the cashier said, without ringing up the bottle.

"You gotta be kidding me, man. I can get a pint of Jameson on the north side for that much. Check how much it is." Colm pointed at the barcode scanner. "I wanna see."

"No, no, no. I want no trouble."

"I ain't starting trouble, bro. I'm your customer and I wanna see what the scanner says." Colm pulled out his wallet. "I'll pay for it. It's just eleven bucks is a lot for a bottle of cheap whiskey."

"No trouble." The cashier waved his hands.

"Bro, I'm not trying to start nothing. I just want to see if eleven is right."

The cashier gave him a dirty look. "Okay."

What a pain in the ass. How hard was it to scan a bottle of whiskey? These guys came here and couldn't even speak English. He wouldn't miss that when he went to Canada.

The cashier slid the bottle over the scanner. The machine rung up a pint of Old Smuggler at $11.01.

"Man...." Colm shook his head. "You guys ain't playing."

"Eleven dollars, one cent," the cashier said.

Colm opened up his wallet. He tried to pull out a twenty, but all the other bills he had stuffed in there came out with it. Money spilled all over the counter.

The cashier's mouth fell open. He said something in Swahili or Arabic or whatever, but Colm didn't understand him.

"Sorry bro." Colm laughed. High quality problems.

He scooped up a handful of bills and stuffed them in the back pocket of his jeans. He pulled a twenty out of the mess on the counter and slid it toward the cashier.

"Don't tell anyone about the money."

The cashier's bug eyes didn't register that he'd heard Colm.

"Guess you couldn't tell anybody if you wanted to." Colm laughed. It wasn't so bad the guy couldn't speak English, after all.

Colm scooped up the rest of the money. He tried to stack it together as best he could, but it fit together like sheets of wet cardboard. He shoved it all in his wallet.

The lone twenty he'd slid across the counter hadn't moved.

"You gonna take that?" Colm pointed at it.

The cashier blinked.

"That's for the whiskey." Colm tapped the bill. "The booze. *Comprende?*"

"Yes," the cashier said. He pulled the bill toward himself, punched 20.00 into the register's keyboard, then laid it in the drawer. He gathered the assortment of crinkled, marked ones and a five, scooped out some change, and held it out for Colm.

"No, that's for you," Colm said. "Keep that."

"No." The cashier shook his head. "You."

"I don't want the change. Put it in your pocket." Colm pantomimed putting something in his pocket so the guy could understand. "Keep it. And take this, too." Colm blindly grabbed a bill out of his pocket, wadded it up, and threw it at him.

"No, sir."

"Yes, sir." Colm didn't have time to argue with this bitch over money. "Take it and keep your mouth shut," he said as he neared the exit.

The automatic door slid open. Colm stepped into the humid, late-June air. People didn't know how brutal the heat could be in Chicago. Even at eleven o'clock at night, it felt like walking into the bathroom while someone took a shower.

He twisted the cap off the whiskey, then he threw it aside. He watched it bounce through the street until it settled in the gutter on the far side, next to a crumpled-up McDonald's bag and an old sneaker.

Colm laughed when he thought of some drunk old bum walking down Ashland Avenue missing a shoe.

He tilted his head back and pulled a mouthful of whiskey out of the bottle.

It felt incredible to drink again, if only for one night. There'd be no booze for him in Canada. Isabella and his unborn kid needed him to be a good man now. He had to get serious, leave his past in Chicago, and be responsible for his new family.

"Sir!"

It was the cashier again.

Colm turned to see him hanging out of the front door. He held up the spare change and the money Colm had lobbed at him.

"Bro, I don't want it," Colm said. "Take it and go back inside. Quit bothering me."

He turned toward the direction of Isabella's house and walked faster.

The cashier didn't say anything in reply. The guy'd finally learned to shut up and accept a good thing.

"Hey, man, you got a cig I can bum?" Someone said from Colm's right. The voice was weird—like the guy was making it lower on purpose. It came from an alley. Colm couldn't quite see him, but he knew it was just some bum.

It was fitting that this city was determined to ruin the first happy night he'd had in years—why change it up now?

"I got nothing for you," Colm said.

"I know you got one," the bum said. He followed behind Colm, matching his footsteps.

"Dude, I already said I ain't got one for you. Now get outta here before I hurt you."

"Come on," the bum said. "Give me a cigarette, Colm."

Colm stopped. He turned around at exactly the right moment to catch an eyeful of muzzle flash.

The light blinded him. The bullet hit him like a mule kick. He stumbled backward and fell, smacking the back of his head on the sidewalk. His vision flashed and his ears rang. He could hardly see. A hot sting lanced his chest and the wetness of his own blood spread across the back of his shirt.

It felt like the bullet caved his entire chest in. Colm gasped for air.

"Sorry man, just business."

Another flash in the darkness.

CHAPTER 2

Chicago had worn Shannon Rourke down to a nub.
An escape from the city was long overdue.

The bodies from all her cases could've stretched
from the front door of her apartment in Wrigleyville to
Lake Shore Drive and back again. Even a CPD detective
had her limits.

She grabbed another pair of socks from the laundry
basket next to her and stuffed them in her duffel bag.
You could never pack too many socks when you went
camping.

A teal bikini top laid in the laundry basket. Shannon
wadded it up and stuffed it in her bag. The lake was
probably warm enough to swim in by now, and Frank
wouldn't forgive her if she didn't get in the water with
him at least once.

Ostensibly, being a detective in the Chicago Police
Department's violent crimes division gave her a 5-days-
a-week, 8-hours-a-day job. In reality, her last day off had

been two months, thirteen cases, and eighteen homicides ago. Some solved, some not.

That's just the way things were.

She'd more than earned herself a long weekend at the Indiana Dunes. And in any case, she felt it was necessary to go say goodbye to the dunes before she and her brother moved to Stockholm and started their lives over.

The Indiana Dunes were her sanctuary—a place where she was able to leave all the baggage of her life behind when she couldn't take anymore.

Anyone outside of Chicago or the region wouldn't believe there were dunes in Indiana. That was what made the place so great. It was a local haven right on Lake Michigan—quaint, quiet, and just happened to be an outstanding national park. Maybe one of the top parks she'd ever been to.

The best part was, as far as Shannon knew, no one had been—or would be—murdered there.

God, she couldn't wait to sit on top of a dune with Frank. They'd watch the sun set over Lake Michigan together—no buildings blocking the horizon, no cars honking or drunk assholes yelling a conversation at each other. Frank would snuggle close to her. She'd put her arm around him. He'd lick her hand, and she'd give him a treat—only after he did a trick, of course.

Giving him a reward he hadn't earned was a gateway to all kinds of behavioral problems. Especially for an American bulldog. They were a sweet breed, but too headstrong. Frank, especially, could get out of hand without strong discipline, even if he loved her to death.

He laid next to her. The long patch of black across his back made him look like an ink stain on the wood floor of her bedroom. He lifted his white chin and looked toward the window, his one white ear standing up straight, his black ear flopped over.

Shannon reached over and scratched his head.

Probably some noise had come from Wrigley and caught his attention. Shannon couldn't hear the Cubs playing through the sounds of El Vy's "Return to the Moon" blasting through her headphones, but if she stuck her head out of her bedroom window, she could just see the top of the stadium lights.

Matt Berninger climbed into his falsetto about Eden Park, then the song cut off.

She had a call from the CPD Area Central Office.

Shannon sighed. She shoved her duffel bag away and looked at Frank. "Should I take it?"

He wagged his tail.

"Guess I have to." She answered the call. "This is Detective Rourke."

"Shannon, we've got a scene down near 46th and Ashland." It was Sergeant Boyd.

"I thought you went home?" she asked.

"I did."

"Doesn't Sergeant Jackson take over the night shift?"

"Her kid's sick."

"So she gets the night off?" Shannon leaned her shoulder up against the foot of her bed. "That doesn't seem entirely fair."

She could hear Boyd simmering on the other side of the call. She shouldn't tease him like this, but how could she help herself when he made it so much fun? Getting a rise out of him was one her favorite pastimes.

"It doesn't matter if it's fair," he said, "there's a job to be done, and I'm doing it. Unfortunately, my job necessitates that I leave a particularly funny Andy Samberg movie about a moronic popstar because I have to lecture a moronic detective about her duty to the city of Chicago."

Okay, that was enough for now. It wouldn't be sporting to make him blow his top too quickly.

"I'm sorry, Boyd." She stuffed back a laugh. "Tell me about the murder."

"There's been a shooting out near a liquor store, and I need you to go take a look at it."

"Okay," she said. "Just to be clear—you know I finished a case today, right?"

"Yes."

"And I haven't had a day off in two months."

He sighed. "Well, Shannon, I know that, but I don't think all the would-be murderers running around the streets of Chicago know about your work schedule yet. If you like, I can try to throw a meeting together."

"That'd be great," she said.

"Okay, I'll put out notices on all the street corners and two-bit strip clubs tomorrow morning. Until then, I need you to get your ass down to 46th and Ashland. This place is called AOK King Liquors."

"Yessir." She pushed herself up off the floor. "My ass is getting down there, sir."

"Good." He ended the call.

She stared at her duffel bag for a moment. So close to getting out for a weekend, but sadly, not close enough. It was a real tragedy.

"You wanna go work this one for me, buddy?" she said to Frank.

He tilted his head and sneezed. His tags rattled.

"I didn't think so."

Shannon walked to her nightstand, then opened the top drawer. She pulled out her keys, her star, and her service weapon—a Glock 17. It was already in her belt holster. She slid the holster over her right hip.

She turned off the lamp on her nightstand. Shannon left her room, and any notion she'd visit the dunes this weekend.

Frank padded ahead of her. His claws clicked on the hardwood floors of her apartment—a reminder that she hadn't walked him nearly enough this week. She'd have to clip his nails before work tomorrow.

She glanced at the clock next to the front door. It was nearly midnight already, and Shannon could feel she'd be out all night. The idea of getting up before work to deal with Frank's hygiene became much less appealing.

He nosed the leash hanging off the coat rack next to the door.

"I can't right now, buddy." She grabbed her work bag off the kitchenette table. "Talk to Michael. He should be back soon."

Frank wagged his white tail.

"Don't stay up." She scratched him under the chin. She loved those prickly little whiskers hiding near his pink lips.

The front door opened behind her. It was Michael.

"Going somewhere?" He had on his Cubs Fukudome T-shirt—a fan favorite.

He was tall enough (and Shannon was short enough) that she had to tilt her head back to look him in the eye when she stood this close to him.

"How'd the Cubs do?"

"They finally got one over St. Louis," he said. "But I think half of Wrigley had already hit the bars by the seventh-inning stretch. Typical Cubs game on a Thursday night. I left The Dugout when it started getting too loud to hear the actual game."

Frank's nose pressed into Shannon's thigh.

"Would you mind taking him out for a walk?" she asked. "I think he's going chew through the walls if someone doesn't put him on the end of his leash."

"I got him." Michael grabbed the leash off the coat rack.

"I'd take him, but work called," she said. "I guess I'm not getting any time off after all."

"I'm sorry." His shoulders sank. He looked almost as upset about it as she was. "I know you needed it."

"Yeah, well, the murderers in this town have quotas to meet, I guess."

Michael laughed. "Everybody's working for somebody."

It made her feel a little better to hear her brother tell a joke. Michael needed his sense of humor more than she did

"Okay, I gotta go. I'll probably be out all night, so don't wait up for me."

"We won't," Michael said.

CHAPTER 3

The blue light from the squad cars flashed half a mile down Ashland.

Shannon parked her old Jeep Wrangler as close as she could get to the crime scene, which had drawn a small crowd of disaffected onlookers needing a distraction, even at this time of night.

The Jeep's parking break groaned into place under her foot. She should've sold the old Wranlger by now, but who could get rid of 2005 TJ? Too many electronics in the new JKs. Anyone with sense knew that.

Its old door creaked shut behind her.

She spotted Detective Dedrick Halman standing near the crime scene cordon tape with a pad of paper in his hand. The sight of him made her heart tap dance a little. He looked like a sharper version of Idris Elba. He was tall, fit and had a smile that could make her sweat if she thought about it too long—it was something about the contrast between his perfectly white teeth and his dark brown skin that grabbed her every time.

Sometimes he made her laugh like a drunk debutante, too.

The little crush she had on him was dangerous for her career, but she couldn't stop herself from feeling it.

She pulled a pair of latex gloves out of her work bag, put them on, then slipped under the tape.

"Hey, Shannon." Dedrick held the same kind of pencil you'd use on a scorecard at a mini-golf place. He was sketching out the crime scene.

"What are doing here?" she asked. "I thought it was my turn to go up to bat."

"If you had an ex-wife blowing up your phone about custody, you'd be out here, too." He traced the sidewalk into his sketch. "Besides, how could I pass up an evening alone with the lovely Detective Shannon Rourke?" He spread a cheesy grin over his face.

She rolled her eyes and pushed a strand of her dark hair behind her ear. "Oh, right," she said. "I look like I just took a bath inside an old garbage can."

He laughed and she pulled a notepad out of her work bag and wrote down the time.

"I need a vacation."

"I thought you had one," Dedrick said.

"I did," she said. "For about six hours."

"Ball-buster Boyd strikes again." Dedrick clicked his teeth. "You ready to go see the body?"

"Sure." Shannon followed him deeper into the crime scene. "When Boyd yanks a vacation away, it stings longer than I thought it would."

"I hear that," Dedrick said. "We were supposed to go to Disney World three years ago—big gesture by me to make the kids happy and show her I wasn't all about the job. But, well, here I am. Anyhow, I thought you might want help with this case before your big move to Stockholm. Figured I could help push it along."

"Oh, God." Shannon pinched the bridge of her nose.

"What?"

"Stockholm," she said. "You know, when Boyd called, Stockholm hadn't occurred to me."

Dedrick put a hand on her back. She felt goosebumps prickle beneath her dark-blue CPD polo.

"Don't worry about it," he said. "When it's time for you to go, I'll take this one over."

"Thanks."

Ahead of them, three men stood in the light spilling out of the doorway to AOK King Liquors. By their outfits, two of them had to be witnesses. The third was Officer Byron Jacobs. He had a legal pad and pen in his hand. A voice recorder rested on the pad, recording the conversation.

"What did Boyd tell you when he called?" Dedrick asked.

"That I had to get my ass down here as quick as I could." The two men were long and lean, both with brushings of tight, black curls on top of their heads. "Do we know anything about the victim?"

"Just what those two told me through Jacobs." Dedrick pointed at them. "They're Congolese. Cousins. They made the 9-1-1 call. The one on the left manages the liquor store, the other one is the cashier—the last person to talk to our victim before he was shot, I'm told. Guess which one doesn't speak a lick of English?"

Shannon snorted.

"Just our luck, isn't it?" Dedrick smiled at her. "Officer Jacobs took a couple years of high school French. The stuff he doesn't understand is explained by the cashier's cousin."

"How much does he understand?" Shannon asked.

"Enough that he could give me the basic details. The victim was shot—quite a bit, apparently. He was white, short-tempered, and came in alone for a pint of Old Smuggler whiskey."

Shannon's throat burned at the thought of Old Smuggler. One of Michael's old friends loved the stuff. When she'd been in high school, she'd been dumb enough to let him pour her a shot. It made her lose her voice for two days and swear an oath to Malibu Rum forever thereafter.

"Anything else?"

"He liked throwing money around," Dedrick said. "The cashier said he wouldn't take his change. The victim threw a twenty at him on his way out the door."

"That's not so bad."

"The Congolese don't take well to charity, I guess."

Shannon furrowed her brow. She didn't know the first thing about the Congo—other than the fact that there were two countries that went by practically the name.

"You don't think the clerk shot him?"

"That's real deep blue of you, Shannon—everybody's a suspect." Dedrick said. "No, I don't think the clerk shot our boy, but I like where your head's at."

"If nobody's innocent, everybody's guilty." She shrugged.

They walked past the Congolese cousins, who were talking faster than Officer Jacobs could possibly understand. Up ahead, an EMT waved off someone who'd stepped too close to the scene from the back of his ambulance.

On the other side of the body, Area Central's newest crime scene tech, Kristof Rud, snapped a picture of blood splatter.

Shannon noticed a brass casing wink at her in the camera flash. It laid inches from the body. There was a small glass bottle, too—a pint of some booze or another.

"The shooter didn't clean up after himself," she said.

"Not this time," Dedrick said. "He didn't leave a weapon for us, at least not one that's immediately obvious. I got a couple uniforms checking the alleys and trashcans nearby."

"Good," Shannon said. "Any idea what the motive was?"

Dedrick sighed. "Who knows with the city the way it is these days? Drugs? Turf? Didn't like his shoes? If those casings weren't there, I wouldn't rule out a random bullet, like what happened to Shimiya Adams."

That name evoked all kinds of bad feelings. Shannon would never forget how the entire department had felt on the night a stray bullet had gone through an open apartment window and killed a little girl making s'mores with her friends. She'd never forget how the city felt. If parents couldn't keep their children safe inside their own homes, no matter how rough the neighborhood, who could ever justify living in Chicago?

"That was stupid to say," Dedrick said. "Sorry, Shannon."

"No, it's all right."

The coroner, Jean DiMarco, leaned up against the ambulance, playing on her cell phone. She lifted her head in Shannon and Dedrick's direction, and waved the both of them over.

"Come to see the body?"

"Regretfully." Shannon watched the red and blue lights skim across the tendril of blood reaching from the body toward the street. "What's the estimated time of death?"

DiMarco pulled a sheet of paper from a clipboard on the ground next to the body. She handed it to Shannon. Right at the top of the page was all the basic information—estimated time of death, suspected cause of death, and the victim's identity, if it could be determined.

As soon as she laid eyes on DiMarco's worksheet, Shannon felt like she'd swallowed concrete.

"Oh my God."

"What?" Dedrick looked at her like she'd sprouted a second head.

"Show me the body," Shannon said to DiMarco.

DiMarco squatted down and folded the sheet back so that the victim's face and upper torso were uncovered.

Shannon's mouth fell open. She knew she should be more professional on a scene, but she couldn't help it. "I have to make a phone call," she said. She turned around and made her way toward her Jeep.

"Shannon, wait."

She only half-heard Dedrick call after her. She elbowed her way through the dozen people gawking at the scene. None of them said anything as she did. Not a one even had the decency to pretend to care about Colm. They were only there to see another body in a city already too full of death.

Don't cry, Shannon. Don't you dare cry.

Her knees began to tremble. Oh, her stupid knees! They'd always been the first part of her to give out. Five miles into her first morning run at Parris, her knees had embarrassed her in front of her DI and all the nervous, homesick recruits who'd barely survived their first night off the bus.

Had her knees thought their knees didn't hurt, too? Weren't they tired? Hadn't they all been through the same things she'd been through? What had made her pain special?

Shannon finally came to a stop on the far side of her Jeep. It was safe here, behind the cover of its tires. She let her weak knees give out. Her palm steadied her on the spit and cigarette-coated sidewalk on the west side of Ashland Avenue.

What in God's name was she going to tell Michael?

She couldn't answer the question. But her other hand reached into the back pocket of her jeans and pulled out her cell phone anyhow. She had to tell her brother something.

It rang twice before Michael answered.

"Hello?" He was groggy, probably lying in bed. Frank's tags rattled in the background. "Shannon?" he asked. "Are you there?"

The words rattled around somewhere in her head before the found footing in her brain and she understood them.

"Yes." She clenched her jaw. No crying. Homicide detectives don't cry. They get mad and they work. They curse the world, they curse human nature, and they bury themselves in case files until their eyes cross.

But they don't cry.

"Shannon? Are you crying?" Michael asked. "What's wrong?"

"Colm," she said. "It's Colm."

"Colm what?" Already, the dread crept into Michael's voice.

"At 46th and Ashland," she said. "He's at my scene."

It took a moment for the meaning of "at my scene" to dawn on him.

"Oh, Jesus," he said.

She swallowed. No blubbering, Shannon. Not in front of Michael. He deserves better from you.

The call went quiet. Impossibly silent, like all the air had been sucked out of Chicago, leaving Shannon and her brother scrambling for a way to speak—as if they ever had much to talk about, despite living together.

"How?" Michael finally asked.

"He was shot," Shannon said. "I'm so sorry, Michael. I didn't know. I didn't see his face until now."

Michael drew a sharp breath on the other end of the call.

"I had to call you as soon as I found out."

"It's okay," he said.

She recognized the familiar sound of Frank licking his face. "Frank, stop it," she said. But she knew the dog couldn't hear her.

For a time, the only sign that Michael hadn't hung up the phone was the sound of Frank trying to comfort him in the only way a dog knew how. At least it was something, and not the choking silence.

"Do you have to take this case?" he asked.

"No." Having a relationship with the deceased not only meant she *could* bow out of the case, but that she *should* bow out.

"Don't take it, then," Michael said. "I know we have to leave soon."

"I know." She wiped away a tear.

"I love you, Shannon," he said.

"I love you, too." She paused for a moment, then took a breath to collect herself.

Then she stood up.

"Make sure Frank stays in your room," Shannon said. "I'll be home late tonight."

"Okay."

She disconnected the call.

Shannon looked back at the scene. Dedrick was halfway between it and her Jeep—frozen, unsure if he should come closer to her or keep his distance. She walked around the hood of her car and waited for him.

He stopped a step short of her. She wanted him to wrap his arms around her and tell her it would be all right. She hoped he couldn't see how bloodshot her eyes were.

"I'll be fine," Shannon said. "You don't have to look at me like that."

"Sure," he said. He looked up at the moon, keeping his eyes away from her. "You knew that man?"

"I grew up with him," she said. "He was my brother's best friend."

Dedrick looked at his shoes. He put his hands in his pockets and his broad shoulders bowed a little. He did his best not to look like he pitied her.

"There's no reason you have to work this case, Shannon," he said. "I'm happy to take this one off your hands. Boyd's fine with it. You know that."

"I do," she said. "But there's *every* reason for me to work this case."

Dedrick sighed. "Detective Rourke, respectfully, as your friend, your co-worker, your colleague—let me have this one. You're too close to this man, and that's going to affect your impartiality. I know how detailed you are in your work, Shannon, and I don't want your feelings to make you miss something, or go after the wrong person." He put a hand on her shoulder. "Let me take this case."

He wasn't going to give this up easily, was he?

"No."

A Marine never gave up, either.

"Don't pull that stubborn soldier-girl hoorah crap on me tonight." Dedrick strained not to raise his voice. "Don't take this case. I'm begging you. You're leaving CPD on a good note. Don't cross it all out at the last minute."

She let her eyes wander to Colm's body. "I owe Michael," she said. "I'm working this case, and there's nothing you can say that'll make me change my mind."

"You *owe* it to your junkie brother?" Dedrick threw his arms up in frustration. "Because last I checked, you told me it was *you* who gave him a place to live, and it was *you* who made him go to twelve-step before he killed himself with heroin. I'm on the outside of whatever's between you two, but it looks to me like he owes you a little more than you owe him."

"You're right," she said. "You are on the outside."

She walked past him. Shannon could do this one fast, and she could do it right, but with a week to solve the case, there was no time for arguing.

For Michael.

CHAPTER 4

"Kid, this one isn't staying in Chicago when you go," Dedrick said.

"Don't call me that." Shannon held her bearing toward Colm's body. "You're only five years older than me."

"I'm thirty-seven, Shannon." Dedrick's hard-soled dress shoes tapped against the asphalt behind her. "That's only four years."

Jean DiMarco stood wide-eyed and grim-faced next to Colm. It was as if she hadn't expected Shannon to come back, like she'd expected her to turn around and run at the first sign of struggle.

"I'd like to examine the body again, please." Shannon stopped just short of a cluster of bullet casings on the sidewalk.

DiMarco looked over Shannon's shoulder—probably at Dedrick—then looked back to Shannon. She crouched down and slowly lifted the covering off Colm's face.

He looked better than she remembered, even given the circumstances of the moment. His red hair was close-shaved to his skull, and the bags he'd always carried under his eyes looked a little shallower than they had when she'd last seen him thirteen years ago.

Apparently, he'd ignored her advice, and the advice of everyone else he knew who had good sense (who could be counted on one hand) and had gotten the tattoos on his neck done. Why anyone would want to see the face of a skeletal marionette peeking out from the neckline of their shirt every time they looked in the mirror, Shannon would never understand.

Then again, Colm was Colm. Stubborn and impulsive as ever.

"Would you show me the wounds, please?" she asked.

Again, Jean looked at Dedrick.

He nodded.

The sheet slipped down past his shoulders. The second she saw Colm's body, she wished she hadn't. She should've listened to Dedrick. She should've started her Jeep, driven home, and cried with her brother.

But she hadn't.

Shannon swallowed a dry lump down her throat and pulled the small flashlight out of the work bag slung over her shoulder. She pushed in the rubber button on its rear and shined it at the gunshot wound in the upper-left quadrant of Colm's chest.

From there, training and routine blocked out her emotions.

The bullet's entry wound was clean. She didn't need to pull off his raggedy t-shirt to see that. And the T-shirt itself had suffered powder burns. The shooter had been close when the trigger was pulled.

Made sense. There was an alley a few steps back and to her right. Probably, he'd ambushed Colm from there.

"Is there an exit wound?" Shannon asked.

"I haven't moved the body yet," Jean said. "I wanted to make sure we had the photos and sketches finished first."

Shannon looked at Rud. He stood a couple paces past Colm's head, staring at her with his camera at chest level.

"Did you get enough shots of the body?"

"Yes—I think so," he said.

"You think so?" she asked. "Did you or didn't you?"

He looked at the screen on the back of the camera, and, presumably, shuffled through his photos. "Yeah," Rud said, "I got it."

"You're sure? Because once we've disturbed this scene, there's no going back to how it was."

"I know." He nodded. "We're good."

Shannon looked at Dedrick. He shrugged.

"Okay," she said. "Let's check for an exit wound."

From close range, there had to be one. That is, unless the shooter was a gun nut, or some kind of weirdo who knew the exact muzzle velocity he needed to ensure the bullet didn't leave Colm's body from close range.

Shannon, Dedrick, and DiMarco rolled Colm onto his side.

The exit wound was slightly lower, just near the bottom of his shoulder blade—so he'd probably been shot by someone taller than him. Shannon guessed Colm was around five-feet, nine-inches tall.

They put Colm on his back. She lifted his shirt and she checked the other wounds. Six in total. There was a cluster of two near his solar plexus, the others were spread out around his chest.

Their exit wounds were higher on his back than the entry points on his front.

"Hold him there for a minute," Shannon said.

Dedrick and DiMarco did as told, keeping Colm rolled up on his right side.

The air was so humid during June in Chicago, the blood under his body hadn't dried yet. It glistened in the flashing lights of the squad cars.

Shannon shined her light into it. Six black spots revealed themselves. They were like small craters in the concrete.

"There they are," she said.

"What?" Dedrick leaned over Colm's body, trying to see what Shannon saw.

"Six impacts in the sidewalk." She pointed at each of them in turn with the bright center ring of her flashlight. They matched the position of the wounds on Colm's torso. "Whoever shot him, they did it while he laid here."

"And they made damn sure he was dead," Dedrick said.

Shannon stood up straight. "You can put him down now."

They rolled him over onto his back again.

"I think the victim and the shooter spoke just before the victim's death," she said. "If Colm came from that liquor store behind us, the position of his head and his feet should be reversed. When he fell on his back, his head should've been pointed toward the liquor store, and his feet should've been pointed away. But they've been switched.

"Maybe the shooter came out of that alley back there." Shannon pointed toward the nearby alley. "Probably said something to the victim to get his attention—maybe something to piss him off, maybe something as simple as asking for a dollar—but he managed to get the victim to turn around and face him."

She held her right arm in front of her as if she aimed a handgun.

"The first shot was close range. The weapon was pointed slightly down, indicating a shooter who is a few inches taller than our victim." She pantomimed recoil from the handgun. "That shot probably knocked the victim down. At some point, the shooter realized he was still alive, or otherwise wanted to make sure he was dead." She stepped forward and aimed the imaginary gun down. "Then he emptied the weapon's magazine into the victim."

Poor Colm. The guy who'd shot him hadn't even had the decency to put a couple in his head.

"Did the officers check that alley?" She pointed with a thumb over her shoulder.

"Probably," Dedrick said. "But if they found anything, they didn't tell me."

Shannon nodded at him. "Let's go."

She walked into the alley first. Dedrick came a couple steps behind her. Both shined their flashlights side-to-side, up and down, looking for anything out of place—anything that might point them one direction or another. There were boxes, a busted-up pallet, and a sweet, rotting smell like a wet dog raised on a steady diet of rotten fruit.

Everything as it should be.

"What're the chances our victim and our shooter knew each other?" Dedrick kicked over an old produce box.

"Pretty good," Shannon said. "At least on paper."

"You know of anyone who'd want your boy dead?"

"He wasn't my boy," Shannon said. "I never really saw him after I enlisted in the Marines."

"Your brother stay in contact with him?"

"Up until a couple years ago, I think," Shannon said. "Colm had a troubled life, and Michael knew he had to get himself away from people like that if he was ever going to stay in recovery."

Up ahead, a shadow moved. Both detectives swung their flashlights to it, ready for anything to come at them—their shooter, an angry bum, the boogieman.

A possum's beady eyes glared back at them.

Dedrick sighed. "What kind of trouble was Colm into?"

"Same kind that Michael was into."

"Drugs?"

"That's not what I meant," she said. "You ever heard of an Irish mobster named Ewan Keane?"

"The name sounds sort of familiar." Dedrick bobbed his head side-to-side, like he was shuffling knowledge around in his brain.

"Ewan is Colm's father."

He lowered his flashlight. The connection wasn't lost on Dedrick—a good detective saw connections in everything.

"Good God, Shannon, you never told me Michael was into something like that," he said.

"He *was*—that's the operative word here," she said. "Michael's out. Has been for years. And last I heard about Colm, he'd been out for a while, too."

"Nobody's ever out," Dedrick said. "You know that's not how those guys work."

"I know I sound naive," she said. "But Michael's out. I keep an eye on him. Nobody comes around to talk to him anymore."

Shannon couldn't read his face in the darkness, but she didn't have to.

Dedrick put his forehead in his hand. Shannon could only imagine how she sounded to him, and what might be going through his mind right now. She couldn't blame him for being leery of how sure she was about her brother. If their roles were reversed, she'd probably take it worse than he was now.

"This is a mess. You know that, right?" he asked.

"I know that."

"And based on the information you just gave me, we should probably call up someone in the Organized Crime Unit. Neither of us should work this case."

She opened her mouth to protest, but he stopped her.

"This goes *so* far beyond the rules, Shannon," he said. "If anyone took a deeper look at this case, they'd see your conflict of interest, and they'd reprimand both of us."

"That's why I need you to keep what I just told you to yourself," she said. "At least until I've got a collar. If we can get the higher-ups the result they want, they don't care how we did it, so long as we can make a charge stick in court."

Dedrick clenched his jaw. He wasn't convinced.

"Come on. All the Organized Crime boys care about are gangs now. You know they don't give a second thought about the Irish Mob," she said. "These aren't the bootlegging days of Capone and the North Side Gang. We throw this case to Organized Crime, and it's tossed into a filling cabinet somewhere because all of their investigative manpower is tied up in drugs and human trafficking."

"They care about murders," Dedrick said.

"If it'll get a conviction on the upper echelons of the Crips or the Latin Kings." She motioned toward the entrance to the alley. "You know this isn't that. This is some small-time punk brazenly gunned down in the street because no one bats an eye if all the Colm Keanes of the world are shot, stabbed, or burnt to keep the United Center warm during a Bulls game."

Dedrick looked back at the squad cars' lights flashing in the street.

She'd made her point. And she knew it was one that would resonate with him. Dedrick hated seeing files pulled down to the Cold Case Unit more than anyone.

"If we do this, you listen to me," he said. "Got it?"

"You know I will."

He shook his head. "No, I don't know that. I know *you*. And I know once you bite into something, you can't let it go."

She shrugged, as if to say, *maybe you're right*.

He stared at her a moment. She liked that he did it in the dark. If she could see his eyes, her crush might force her to soften up on him.

"You're lucky," he said. "You realize that, right?"

"How am I lucky?"

"Because if you were a fat, sweaty homicide detective like Jorge Goyez, I wouldn't put up with nearly as much from you—my life would be far less complicated if you weren't pretty."

Her cheeks flushed. Even the darkness wasn't safe, apparently. She turned her eyes away from Dedrick. She had to get a grip on herself—Colm's body lay, cold, a few feet off.

And when she looked away, Shannon noticed something on the ground, just at the edge of her flashlight's reach. She centered on it. A cigarette butt peeking around the far side of a dumpster.

She stepped toward it.

"What is it?" Dedrick said.

"Look." She pointed at it.

He put his flashlight on it, too. "A cigarette butt." He didn't sound impressed. "You got any roaches or rats you want to point out to me while you're at it?" Shannon stepped around the far side of the dumpster. She found a half-dozen more. A crumpled Marlboro Red hard pack lay nearby, too.

She was careful to step over them. Shannon pressed her back up against the brick wall, then crouched down to see if she could hide behind the dumpster with the pile of spent cigarettes at her feet.

"They're probably just from some bum," Dedrick said.

"You think somebody who can barely afford a cup of coffee would smoke that much of a twelve-dollar pack of cigarettes in one sitting?"

"Maybe he was a rich bum." Dedrick shrugged. "How do you know it wasn't someone taking a smoke break?"

"Do you see any doors in this alley?" She shined the light up and down the brick walls on either side. "Who goes more than ten feet away from a door when they smoke? Who would hide behind a dumpster?"

Dedrick shined his light down the alley one last time, looking for something to disprove Shannon's theory.

"All right, detective," he said. "Let's tag 'em."

Shannon took out her smartphone and snapped a couple photos before she disturbed the evidence. She'd hand them off to Rud later for filing.

With that taken care of, she pulled a plastic baggie out of her shoulder bag and scooped the cigarettes into them. If they could get a decent print from the pack and a decent print from the bullet casings, they might be able to make somebody on this.

Shannon emerged from the alley, feeling a little surer of the case's direction.

"Would you like me to take his body to the morgue now, Detective?" Jean DiMarco screwed the lid on a vial containing a bloody cotton swab. She'd already covered Colm below his shoulders with the sheet. "I believe I've got all I can use."

It was better not to look into Colm's eyes, but Shannon couldn't stop herself.

Even closed, and even in death, his eyes had a wild undertone to them. They carried the look of a boy who would take a left turn at any moment; who gleefully jumped into fistfights with his friends, whether they were wrong or right; a boy who drove his car through the neighbors' yards for a cheap laugh, and who'd throw you a beer before the first bell whether he liked you or just wanted to see you get in trouble.

Sure, Colm had been an asshole. He'd have told you so himself.

But he hadn't deserved to die.

And Shannon wouldn't leave her brother saddled with the grief of never knowing why someone had decided his old friend Colm deserved to have an entire clip emptied into him.

"Take him to the morgue," Shannon said. "I'm going to inform the next-of-kin."

CHAPTER 5

Addison, Illinois slept outside the western reaches of Chicago. Fifty minutes away from the liquor store, according to Shannon's GPS. She made it in thirty-nine.

"You ever think about what driving like that does to your car?" Dedrick stepped out of the Jeep and onto Jill Keane's front lawn. He twisted his chin over his left shoulder, cracking his neck. "Not to mention my nerves."

"He's good for it."

Shannon grabbed her work bag, then closed the tailgate as lightly as she could. People in the suburbs were touchy about noises outside their homes at four in the morning.

"Your car is a man." Dedrick shrugged. "Why not?"

She rolled her eyes.

"I'm not judging." He put his hands up and smiled. "Only observing."

Shannon lifted her eyebrows at him. Eventually, that cute smile of his would wear out its welcome—but probably not any time soon.

Across the manicured lawn ahead of them, a porch light flicked on. A curtain behind the big-picture window on the front of the house swayed as if someone peeked out.

"At least we won't have to knock very hard," Dedrick said.

The front door flew open. Behind the porch light, the figure of a tall, thin man appeared.

"You two better turn around and walk away." The rack of a shotgun punctuated the man's warning. "I don't see any reason why you think you can come up to my house at this time of night."

Did every nut in the suburbs lay awake in bed with their Mossberg 500 across their chest?

Both Shannon and Dedrick drew their weapons.

"Sir, put the weapon down!" Shannon yelled from behind her Glock. She really wasn't in the mood to blow away some idiot who was too quick to point a gun.

"Drop the gun, moron!" Dedrick yelled. "We're the police."

"If you're the cops, show me your badges."

Shannon unclipped her star from the front pocket of her jeans. She held it out.

"Can't see it," the man said. "Hold it up higher."

"We're two detectives here to talk about your son," Dedrick yelled at him. "We just want to speak with Jill—put the gun away."

"I don't have a son." He kept his shotgun pointed at the ground. "Show me your badge, pretty boy."

Dedrick thrust his hand into the inside of his jacket and pulled out a leather wallet. His star was clipped to the front.

"Good," the man said. "Now put your badge up higher, sweetheart."

In that instant, Shannon's willingness to play this dumb game vanished.

"That was the wrong word to use, man," Dedrick said.

"You calling me sweetheart?" She stuffed her star in her pocket. "How's this for a sweetheart? If you don't put that shotgun down *now*, sir, I'm going to shoot you. Is that sweet enough for you?"

He blinked at her. "I—uh … I'm a citizen," he half-whispered. "I don't have to stand for this tyranny."

The thin man in the doorway kept his shotgun pointed down. Smart of him. If he pointed it at her, she'd shove that thing so far up his ass, he'd have buckshot for teeth.

"You pointed the gun at us first," Dedrick said. "Now put the damn thing down."

"I know my rights! This is an unlawful search of my domicile, and the Fourth Amendment forbids it!"

"And you're brandishing a weapon at a law enforcement officer." With her Glock drawn and aimed straight at his neck, Shannon moved up the lawn.

He held his ground inside the open front door. But he wasn't all that brave. She'd spent enough time around people who truly were. She knew the fakers as soon as she smelled them.

"I don't like weapons brandished at me." She clomped up the front porch's concrete steps. It felt like the house shivered for a moment. "Especially when I haven't done anything to deserve it."

She reached for him. Grabbing the shotgun halfway down the barrel, she swept it aside and wrenched it out of his hands at the same time.

She pulled back the pump on the shotgun. A shell hopped out.

"Is that birdshot?"

"I, uh … yes."

Shannon rolled her eyes at him. She pumped the Mossberg four more times until there were shells scattered all over the wicker chair sitting to the right of the door.

She tossed the Mossberg at him. He caught it.

"Now that we've taken care of that little moronic display, would you go get your wife?" she asked.

"Y-Yes, ma'am." He scurried off.

Dedrick laughed behind her. His shoes tapped up the concrete walk. "I couldn't tell if he was going to blow your head off, or blow off his own to get away from you."

She turned to scowl at Dedrick—now wasn't the time for kidding around. But she saw the shotgun shells scattered on the wicker chair's floral-patterned seat and couldn't stop from losing herself.

Who wouldn't laugh at that?

She bellowed laughter. Long and hard. The neighbors must've thought a loon was on the prowl. Maybe they weren't wrong.

When Shannon looked up, the house and the Chicago suburbs were gone.

A tan canvas tent surrounded her. The Mesopotamian sun bled through it, warming her skin. The tent was big enough to house a platoon, but there was only one other person here.

AJ lay, naked, on a pair of cots they'd shoved together. He stared at the ceiling, then he moved his head like he heard something.

He rolled over onto his stomach and smiled at her. His rubber-rimmed dog tags dropped off the edge of the cots, to dangle from around his neck.

"Damn fine idea to bring birdshot here." He smiled and tossed one of the green shells from hand to hand. "I bet we can sneak away from the war. Maybe go to Basrah in a humvee and hunt crake."

Her heart ached in her chest. It'd been at least ten years since she'd seen him.

He tossed the shotgun shell at her. It hit her in the chest like a brick, and knocked her back. She closed her eyes and fell.

"Shannon?"

Her eyes opened. She wasn't quite sitting and wasn't quite standing. Dedrick had her propped up by her shoulders.

The cute little suburban house was back.

"I'm fine," Shannon said. She got to her feet with Dedrick's help. "Just a little too tired."

She blinked until her eyes focused on the weathered-looking Irish woman in front of her.

Jill Keane held the top of her robe closed with one hand. She scowled at Shannon from across the threshold of her front door.

"Mrs. Keane," Shannon said. "You may not remember me, but my name is Shannon Rourke—I'm a detective with the Chicago PD, Area Central. My brother, Michael, was a friend of Colm's, and I'd like to speak with you about him, if that'd be all right."

"I'm Detective Dedrick Halman, Mrs. Keane—I'm working with Detective Rourke tonight."

She stared at them. The thin line of her mouth stood pat. Her eyes looked like they would slice the two of them to bits if they said the wrong thing.

"Would you mind if we spoke to you about Colm, Mrs. Keane?" Dedrick asked.

"It's Tiller now," Jill said. Forty years away from the Irish isle, and she still carried the specter of an accent.

"Pardon?"

"It's Mrs. Tiller, now. I married David two years ago," she said.

"Oh," Dedrick said. "Of course."

"Can we come in?" Shannon asked.

"If you think it's worth the time," she said. "Don't know that I really want to talk about anything Colm has done."

Shannon exchanged a look with Dedrick. They wiped their shoes on the doormat outside the house before they came in. Dedrick closed the front door behind them.

The smell inside the Tillers' home reminded Shannon of her aunt's house at Easter. The walls were white, the family pictures were plentiful—though Shannon guessed most of them belonged to David—and it seemed that Jill Tiller had a weakness for floral prints. The couch was floral, the curtains were floral, and if Shannon cared to check the bathroom, she'd guess the walls were done up in paper with prints of snapdragons, black-eyed Susans, dahlias, and all the rest.

"You can have a seat," Jill said, motioning toward the couch.

"I'm gonna make some coffee." David sulked his way into the kitchen. Shannon couldn't help but take a little joy from his sour mood—though he should've been in better spirits. Not many people pointed a gun at CPD officers and walked away without a bullet for their troubles.

"How's your brother getting along these days?" Jill asked Shannon.

"Fine," she said. "He's probably bored, but he could do with a little boredom."

Jill nodded. She understood. "Not surprised to hear he's lived fast—but I am a little taken to see that you're a police officer," she said. "At the end of it all, you're both Tommy Rourke's children."

Shannon hadn't heard her father's name in some time. Years, if she was lucky.

"You could say that," Shannon said. "Though Tommy wasn't much of a family man."

"He loved to drink," Jill said. "God rest his soul."

Shannon gave her a tight smile.

It wouldn't be right to snap at Jill, though she wanted to. She meant well. But if there were a God in Heaven, he'd have overnighted Tommy Rourke's soul to Hell where he'd serve out eternity running laps around Satan's hottest bonfire.

The son of a bitch deserved the worst for what he'd done to Michael all those years—and what he'd tried to do to Shannon.

"So, what have you come to ask me about Colm?" Jill asked. "Out working for his father again?"

Shannon grimaced. *Maybe he was*, she wanted to say. *And what would you know about it, Mrs. Tiller?*

It could wait. There wasn't much tact in interrogating a woman moments before you told her about her son's murder.

"Mrs. Tiller," she said, "I've come with bad news about Colm."

Jill's expression dropped, but she kept eye contact with Shannon.

"He was shot," Shannon said. "We found his body over near 46th and Ashland."

She sighed, then she scrunched the corners of her mouth. She nodded. "I see."

"Mrs. Tiller," Dedrick said, "do you understand what Detective Rourke just told you?"

"Yes," she said. "And I'd like to point out that neither of you knew Colm like I did. He was an ungrateful son—a little monster. If I'm surprised at all, it's because he should've gotten himself killed years ago."

She cleared her throat. Sitting up, she grabbed a pack of cigarettes from the side table next to her chair—Newports. She flipped open the top and picked one out.

"What makes you say that?" Shannon asked.

"Oh, Shannon, really." Jill lit the cigarette and took a puff. "You knew him growing up. You knew how quick-tempered he was. How he'd wreck and ruin anything he could get his hands on if it suited him. Imagine having to live with that every day. But by the grace of God have I held onto any of my sanity."

The poor woman. Colm's antics had worn on Shannon at times. Like when he'd stolen her bookbag in high school, rummaged through it, then tossed all her tampons into the hallway.

"Did you know anyone who'd want to kill him?" Dedrick clicked his pen.

"Not really, no." Jill ashed her cigarette into a faded Mickey Mouse coffee cup. "I didn't speak with him much after the divorce."

"But you did speak to him?" Dedrick said.

"He'd call. Mostly when he thought he could get something from me—money, usually." She shrugged and exhaled a cloud of cigarette smoke. "We talked around last Easter. I remember it because he said he was turning his life around. But for me, it was too late. I wished him well and went back to making my deviled eggs. I didn't want to be taken into his antics again."

Shannon jotted down some key points on her notepad.

"When were you and Ewan divorced?" she said.

"Ten years ago last month." Jill tapped the end of her cigarette into her Mickey Mouse cup again.

"Mind if I ask why?"

"Tommy Rourke's daughter asking me why Ewan and I divorced?" She took a drag from the cigarette. "Yes, I mind."

"What if I ask?" Dedrick said. "I'm the son of nobody you know—my dad ran a gas station in Tuscaloosa."

Jill looked him over. "I don't think my divorce has anything to do with Colm's death."

"Probably not," Shannon said. "But you never know."

Jill chuckled. "I liked you better when you were younger. You weren't so nosy."

"Yeah, well, we all change, don't we?" Shannon said.

"Not in my experience," Jill said. "When you try to go around changing who you are, it's like trying to shoo off your own shadow. It doesn't go away easy like that. It stays right beside you, no matter if you like it or not."

"Is that why you didn't think Colm could make himself a better person?" Shannon asked.

"You tell me." Jill tapped out the cigarette. "You're the people trying to figure out why someone would kill him."

Shannon sighed and put down her pen and pad of paper. She looked at Dedrick in an unspoken invitation to take things over if he felt like it.

"Look, Mrs. Tiller. Jill," he said. "Clearly you and your husband don't care for our being here. And you seem at peace with your son's death. So, if you would just tell us anything you know about Colm—his recent where-abouts, who he spent time with, where he worked—we'd appreciate the info, and we'll move on."

She took another cigarette out of the pack. The faint smell of menthol touched Shannon's nose.

"He didn't work." She lit it. "My son was a deadbeat."

"Do you have his most-recent home address?" Shannon asked.

Jill looked at Shannon from the side of her eyes. "I'll get my address book."

She walked across the living room, toward the hallway between the front door and the couch where Shannon and Dedrick sat, then disappeared.

Shannon waited until she couldn't hear the soft shuffle of Jill Tiller's slippers against the hallway carpet before she spoke up.

"In the five years I've done this job, I've never seen anyone react to their child's death like that unless they had some part to play in it," she said.

"Even the guilty parents ham it up when the police come by asking questions," Dedrick said.

He was right.

"What're the odds she leaves us sitting here while she goes back to bed?" he asked.

"Decent enough that I wouldn't bet against it." Shannon stood up from the couch. She had to move around or risk falling asleep right here in the Tillers' living room.

Jill had left her cigarette burning in the ashtray. Shannon picked it up, then snubbed it out. "Terrible habit."

"You aren't getting on anyone's good side around here," Dedrick said.

"They started it."

David Tiller returned from the kitchen with a mug of steaming coffee.

Shannon looked over the edge of the mug. Black coffee. Anyone who said they enjoyed black coffee was a liar. You couldn't enjoy anything that tasted like chalk.

"I have a question, Mr. Tiller," she said.

His eyes met hers as he slurped his coffee. "How did you know Detective Halman and I were on your front lawn?"

"I was awake," he said as he sat down in his over-stuffed leather recliner. "Couldn't sleep."

"Probably hard to sleep with a shotgun under your pillow," Dedrick said.

"Easier than you might think." David took another slurp of his coffee. "All those gangs out there in Chicago make me nervous."

"You get many gangbangers out this far?" Dedrick asked.

"No," David said. "But I keep wondering when they're finally going to come my way and ruin the neighborhood. You know they're out there, looking at my house and my car and wondering when they can take it."

"I don't think they can see all the way to Addison from around Humboldt Park," Dedrick said.

David Tiller sneered at him. "You think you're so damn funny, but cops like you are part of the problem. You think you can barge into a man's house and kick him around at any old time of night." He edged forward in his chair. "I'm a law-abiding citizen, sir. I know my rights."

"Yes, we know," Shannon said. "You demonstrated your mastery over Constitutional Law earlier."

He spit out a little disgusted air. He sank into his chair.

"Here's Colm's address." Jill stepped out from the hallway. She stabbed a piece of paper at Dedrick. "Take it and leave, please."

Dedrick stood up, adjusted the waist of his pants, then took the slip of paper from her hand. He read it out loud.

"1717 North Albany Avenue, #2." He looked at Jill. "Is this an apartment?"

"How would I know?" Jill asked. "I told you I didn't much care for Colm."

Many times over.

Shannon grabbed her bag and made her way to the door. Dedrick followed, as did David Tiller.

When she and Dedrick stood on the porch of the Tillers' home, she looked to her left and grabbed one of the twelve-gauge birdshot shells. She tossed it to David.

"You might want that back," she said.

The front door slammed closed behind her.

CHAPTER 6

North Albany Avenue was nothing special at six in
the morning. It wasn't the Indiana Dunes. It wasn't
sunlight breaking over Lake Michigan, stealing
the breath out of Shannon while she scratched Frank
under his collar. It was a little street north of Humboldt Park where people parked their modest cars
out front of their modest town homes.

Colm Keane's townhouse fit right in with the rest of
them. At least, it looked that way from his front porch.

"Doesn't look like what I had in my head," Dedrick
said. "I expected something a little ... rougher."

"Hold your judgments until we see the inside."
Shannon tried to shield the glass of Colm's front window
from the growing sunlight so she could peek inside. But
a cheap venetian blind hung cockeyed across the other
side of the glass.

"Think he lived with anyone?" Dedrick asked. "Roommate or something?"

"Your guess is as good as mine."

He knocked on the front door again. Nothing moved inside Colm's house.

"Guess we should call in a warrant," Dedrick said.

"I'll go grab my phone out of the car."

Shannon had started down the front steps when the next-door neighbor stepped outside. He was tall, in his twenties, and had dark brown hair, an angular face, and the lean, muscular body of a sworn gym rat. He probably thought the world owed him something he hadn't earned, and he was mad about it. He fit the mold, at least.

"Y'all looking for Colm?" he asked.

She stopped. "What makes you say that?"

He motioned toward the star hanging off her front pocket. "Always got the impression that dude was into something."

"Really?" she said. "Would you mind if I asked you a couple questions about him?"

He grimaced and scratched the back of his head. He wasn't taking her attention too well. He looked nervous enough to shrivel up and disappear inside his jeans and baggy T-shirt.

"All right," he said.

"What makes you think he was into anything illegal?"

"Dude had a look to him. The kind of look y'all probably seen a thousand times a day," he said. "Know what I mean?"

Shannon knew.

"What's your name, sir?" she asked.

"Robbie."

"You have a last name, Robbie?" Dedrick asked from the porch.

"Simmons." He pointed at a maroon Toyota Camry parked across the street. "I was about to leave for my job, but I got a couple minutes for y'all."

Shannon approached the chest-high picket fence between Robbie's yard and Colm's. It was in bad need of some TLC. She leaned her forearms on it and contained her amazement that it didn't crumble under her putting the slightest bit of weight on it.

"How well did you know Colm Keane?"

"I dunno," Robbie said. Beads of sweat sparkled on his forehead. "Guess I'd say 's'up to him if I saw him outside."

"That's it?" Shannon asked.

"Yeah."

"Why would you think he was a criminal?"

Robbie shied away from the detectives for a moment. "I shot my mouth off. I should've minded my own business, I know. But I ain't mean nothing by it." Robbie licked his lips. "If y'all are cool with it, I don't want to be late for work again."

"Hold on," Shannon said. Why was he being so skittish all of a sudden? "When was the last time you saw Colm?"

"I really gotta go." He fidgeted with the keys in his pocket.

"We'll write you a note," Dedrick said. "Answer her questions."

Robbie looked at Shannon and sighed. "Last time I saw Colm was yesterday, I guess."

"When yesterday?" She shifted her weight on the fence. The post beneath her creaked.

"Afternoon? Evening maybe?"

"Any clue what was he doing?"

"I dunno." He rubbed the back of his neck and looked at his shoes. "I wasn't really paying him no mind. I just got off work, and I wanted to go inside and get a drink."

"And where did you say you worked?"

"The CTA." Robbie pulled out his cell phone and checked the time. "I gotta get going, man."

"We'll make sure you don't get in trouble," Shannon said. "I just have a couple more questions."

Robbie cocked his eyes at her dubiously. "I ain't see how y'all can make that happen."

She looked at Dedrick and held out her hand. He fished out a business card from his inside coat pocket and gave it to her.

"If your supervisor or your manager or anyone else wants to know why you were late, you have them call us at this number." She gave Robbie the card. "CPD won't let your boss interfere with a murder investigation."

Robbie's eyes popped open. "You telling me Colm murdered somebody?"

Dammit. She hadn't meant to let that slip out—at least not in that way.

"No," Shannon said.

It took a second for Robbie to process what that meant. When he did, his knees buckled. He dropped onto the cracked walk leading from his house and he covered his face with his hands.

"I can't believe it." His voice strained like he barely held back tears. "I just can't, man. That dude got killed?"

Shannon didn't know what to tell him. Anything she wanted to say wouldn't have helped. She stayed quiet.

"Y'all tell his family?" Robbie rubbed at his eyes. He had a rose tattooed on the back of his right hand, and it shivered with his spasmodic breathing.

"We told his mother. We haven't contacted his father yet," Shannon said. "Are you going to be okay, Mr. Simmons?"

"Yeah, I'll be fine." Robbie rubbed his hand through his hair. He had a look on his face like he was waffling between pulling himself together and scattering his body into the winds for Lake Michigan. He finally said, "Yeah."

Dedrick tapped Shannon on the shoulder and jerked his head toward Robbie. He wanted to press forward with questioning him, and she couldn't think of a reason why they shouldn't.

"I don't want to minimize your pain," Dedrick said, "but I'm thinking you knew Colm a little better than you admit."

Robbie's gaze shot up to Dedrick. "I dunno. I mean, I knew the dude, yeah."

"He wasn't just your neighbor," Dedrick said. "You two were tight."

Robbie shrugged.

"I know you're grieving and all, but you've got to tell us the truth."

"I ain't lied to y'all!" Robbie jumped to his feet. "Tell him I ain't lied to you," he said to Shannon. He appeared to bounce out of his grief extraordinarily fast.

Dedrick stepped off Colm's front porch in that slow, thoughtful, and dangerous way that only a man his size could. He let the weight of his mood, his inner monologue, become known through long and heavy steps up to the fence, next to Shannon.

"Mr. Simmons, the State's Attorney doesn't have much sympathy for people who lie to police officers conducting an investigation," Dedrick said. "So I'm going to give you one last chance to tell us the God's honest truth."

"I did!" Robbie said.

"We know somebody came by looking for him!"

Dedrick was bluffing. But both he and Shannon knew Robbie had more information about Colm than he shared. They'd find a way to shake it loose.

"Tell us!" Dedrick bellowed. "Tell us before I have to drag your ass back to station."

Robbie recoiled from Dedrick. He looked to Shannon for help—a good sign. He trusted her and was afraid of Dedrick, just as they liked it.

"I can't help you if we find out you knew something you didn't tell us," Shannon said.

Robbie looked back to Dedrick, trying to get a read on him. "Couple dudes came by," Robbie said.

"When?" Dedrick asked.

"Three nights ago."

"They looking for Colm?

Robbie nodded.

"Did you get a look at them?"

"It was dark," Robbie said. "All I saw was two old white guys."

"How old?"

He shrugged. "I dunno—old."

"About what age?" Dedrick was on the verge of losing his temper again. Shannon put a hand on his back to calm him down.

"Forties?" she asked. "Fifties? Older?"

"Fifties." If Robbie had hair on his back, it would be standing on end. "One tall, one short."

"That's all?" Dedrick's fingers gripped the fence so hard, his nails went white.

"I said it was dark, man—I couldn't hardly see nothing."

"What lie are you going to tell us next?" Dedrick asked. "You didn't hear anything because you had your earmuffs on?"

"All right, Detective," Shannon said. She grabbed him by the shoulder. She turned her back to Robbie as she ushered Dedrick away. "Let's take a breather here. Let me talk to Robbie alone for a minute."

"If he tries to keep playing stupid," he said quietly, "call him white boy. I always wanted to hear you call somebody white boy."

Shannon rolled her eyes. "Settle down."

"If you know what's good for you, you'll answer Detective Rourke's questions," Dedrick yelled at Robbie. "If you don't—remember, I'll be waiting for you with a nice, new pair of bracelets."

Shannon smiled and playfully pushed Dedrick back toward his car.

The smile dissolved the instant she turned around, and her face was visible to Robbie. She walked back to the old fence. It sagged where Dedrick had rested his hands on it. Robbie's eyes were glued to that little section of rickety one-by-four boards.

"I apologize for Detective Halman," Shannon said.

"Dude better lay off the 'roids," Robbie said. "I'm just trying to help y'all and he's getting all crazy with me."

"Believe it or not, I think he appreciates that you came clean," Shannon said. "We both know you want to help Colm."

"It's cool," Robbie said. "I just ain't trying to get my head ripped off by nobody."

"I understand," she said. "Now, you told us there were two men who paid Colm a visit the other day. How long did they stay? Did it look like Colm knew them?"

"They were here a couple minutes," Robbie said. "And, yeah, it looked like he knew them. When he answered the door, they ain't hardly said a word to him before he started screaming at them."

Shannon pulled her notebook out of her bag. "What about?"

"I dunno, I was sitting on my front porch, so I couldn't hear all that well. Sounded like they was arguing about money or something."

She wrote down, "argument, money" on the pad of paper just below the address Jill Tiller had given her. "If you couldn't hear them, how'd you know they argued over money?"

He snorted. "Ain't much of anything else people get that heated about."

"Women, drugs, sports," Shannon said.

"Yeah, I guess you're right," Robbie said. "Maybe when I think about it, I heard the word 'money' a couple times. Like those two dudes saying Colm owed them."

"Do you think Colm owed them?"

He looked at Colm's front porch and shrugged. "I ain't seen his pocketbook, if that's what you mean."

"How about this," Shannon said. "You ever see him throwing money around? Maybe having a couple parties here, wearing nice clothes—stuff like that."

"Nah," Robbie said. "I mean, you can look through his front window and see there ain't nothing in that house worth more than a few bucks. I don't even know if Colm had a TV."

"Wait a minute," she said. "If you never really hung out with Colm, how do you know so much about what the inside of his house looks like?"

Robbie froze. He'd made a misstep, and Shannon hadn't missed it.

"Me and Colm would head out every now and again," he said. "But it wasn't like we were boys or nothing. Just neighbors who like going to the same bars."

Suddenly, Robbie's expression changed.

"You look like somebody walked over your grave," Shannon said.

"I remembered something," Robbie said. "He been throwing money around."

She looked at him, waiting for more.

"We'd walk to McCollough's Pub over on Albany sometimes. You know, just to chill or whatever. Last time we was there, he was buying like he won the lottery — shots, beers, whatever. He was laying drinks on anybody coming through the door. Didn't matter if it was a dime or some crusty old dude, Colm bought their drinks. Dude racked up a tab like I ain't seen anybody do before, and didn't trip over it. I was a couple drinks in by the end of the night, but I remember watching him pay for the bill with straight cash."

Shannon clicked her pen a few times. She narrowed her eyes at Robbie. "You forgot about that?"

"I was lit that night," he said. "I'm lucky I can remember my own name."

"You seem a tad forgetful," Shannon said. "Anybody ever tell you that?"

He shrugged. "Ain't every day I get two cops asking me questions."

No, probably not. But Robbie looked like a kid who'd seen his fair share of cops.

"I think I've got all I need here," Shannon said. "I appreciate your time, Robbie. Can I count on you being here if I have any follow-up questions?"

"Yeah," he said. "And next time, if you wanna come around without him—" he pointed at Dedrick "—that's cool with me. A woman like you'd get a lot more out of me than he would." Robbie smiled at her.

Shannon smiled back. Better to let him think she liked him than not. She could feel his eyes studying her butt as she walked back to Dedrick, who leaned up against her Jeep with his hands in his pockets. Mr. Cool himself.

"What'd he say?" Dedrick inclined his head at Robbie as he crossed the street in front of his house.

She filled him in on the details while Robbie pulled past in his Camry. Dedrick stared him down until the car pulled out of sight.

"I think our next move is to get a warrant," Shannon said. "We need to check Colm's house for any evidence that he owed someone money or otherwise had a large sum of it."

"You believe what he told you?"

"It's worth checking out. Somebody wanted Colm dead, and he gave us a working theory as to why. In any case, I think it's wise to get a marked car to watch Colm's house until we can get our warrant."

"All right, kid," Dedrick said. "You call in a patrol unit, and I'll get to work on the warrant while you get some sleep."

The mention of sleep sent her into a yawning fit.

"I'm not taking a nap," Shannon said. "We've got a lot of work to do."

"I can handle it on my own." He pulled open the passenger door on her Jeep and got inside. "You've got an eight-hour vacation to take—that is, after you run me back to my car over on Ashland."

"I can't make you work on the warrant alone." Shannon rubbed her eyes. Dammit, all it took was the thought of a break and her body went into a full-on mutiny.

"It isn't like you can type on one-half of my keyboard while I type on the other—you're exhausted, Shannon. Take the morning off and come back around two. You're useless without sleep."

She lightly punched his knee. He smiled at her.

"I went without sleep way longer than this in the Corps," she said.

"I know. You're a real tough gal," he said. "Now take me back to my car and go get some rest."

"You know," she said, "you're a lot less entertaining when I haven't slept."

CHAPTER 7

The morning rush hour in Chicago was not something to trifle with. After heading south from Colm's townhouse and dropping Dedrick off at his department-issued Chevy Impala, Shannon had to double-back to Wrigleyville.

She didn't get home until ten AM—a full two and half hours after she and Dedrick left Colm's place.

By the time she opened the door to her upstairs apartment, her brain almost couldn't figure out which key went into the lock. Maybe she'd gone without sleep when she was nineteen, but at age thirty-one, she couldn't do it anymore. Through sheer force of will, she solved the problem. She stabbed the lock with the key, turned the knob, and practically fell through the doorway.

Thankfully, Frank was there to steady her.

He jumped up to greet her, as he sometimes did, and as she sometimes told him not to. He stretched his paws up to her chest and leaned into her. His tongue swiped at the bottom of her chin.

"Hi, buddy." She scratched him between the ears. "Now, get down."

Frank relented. He sat down, his tail sweeping the front doormat.

"Good boy."

He stood, then nosed the leash hanging off the coat rack to her left, then looked at her.

"Maybe we'll go out a little later," she said. "I've been running around the city all night."

He sneezed and shook his head. He wouldn't give up that easily.

Neither would Shannon. The two of them made a good match like that. Frank would've pushed around some sweet old lady looking for a big dog, and he would've had the run of any middle-class family who dared take him in, thinking he'd be nice for the kids.

He touched his nose to the leash again.

"After I sleep," she said, and made her way toward her room.

Frank didn't follow. In the past, he would stand at the door and use the tip of his nose to bat at the leash for hours at a time. He always tired of that eventually, at which point he'd crawl into her bed and sleep until his next chance at a walk.

She passed by Michael's room. His door was open a crack.

"Michael?" Shannon pushed it open slowly.

Her brother lay on top of the sheets of his bed in the same Fukudome T-shirt he'd worn last night. He was asleep. His laptop sat open next to him.

He was too big for her to move, so she went back to the living room to grab a blanket to cover him with. Frank gave her a dirty look when she dared show her face without grabbing the leash off the wall.

Shannon's old comforter—a light-colored, plaid blanket she'd had since middle school—was on the couch. She grabbed it, went back to Michael, and laid it on top of him.

That's when she noticed his computer was open to Facebook. Colm Keane's page, to be exact. She leaned closer to it and read people's notes to him. It appeared that word of his death had gotten out.

She wasn't surprised. Maybe Michael had let others know after she'd called him last night.

Shannon knelt at the side of his bed. She scrolled the page down a bit, looking at Colm's old updates, hoping something would take hold of her. Maybe he'd left a trail of what he'd been up to, or someone had location tagged him somewhere significant.

She stopped.

A picture she recognized was on the laptop's screen. She remembered the moment one of Michael's friends had taken it. She couldn't remember the kid's name (was it Jimmy, or Jason?) but she remembered the old railroad bridge they all used to hang out under when they were teenagers.

Colm sat on a concrete footing which held up the bridge. He raised his Coors Light up high, smiling wide. Michael leaned up against the same footing, his beer tucked in to his folded arms. He had that signature smirk on his face—the one all the girls in Shannon's class had loved. Shannon sat cross-legged in the yellowed grass beneath the bridge, tagging along with her brother, for fear of being left home alone when her father came back stinking drunk.

Drinking stolen beer under the railroad tracks at sixteen. A little sadness choked her. Had Michael ever had a chance?

He turned in his sleep.

There was nothing new to learn about Colm here.

Shannon put his laptop back the way she found it. She closed the door behind her, softly as she could.

Across the hall, Frank laid in front of her door. He lifted his head and wagged his tail when she looked at him. It whacked against the wall loud enough that she was afraid Michael would wake.

"Come on, knucklehead." She opened her bedroom door, and Frank slipped in with her.

With her heavy curtains drawn, not a shaft of sunlight entered the room. She'd worked enough late nights on CPD's behalf to know that blackout curtains were a wise investment.

She heard Frank jump up on her bed. Then she nearly tripped over her half-packed duffel bag.

Shannon groaned and kicked it across the room. No chance she'd get to go to the dunes now, but that was fine. She'd be in Stockholm soon, and when she was, everything would be perfect.

She fell face first into her bed, thoughts of flights and jobs and getting the hell out of Chicago swirling around her head.

Frank snuggled up next to her hip.

CHAPTER 8

There was something charmless about waking up to the sound of a ringing phone.

Her phone's vibrations shook the entire bed from the front pocket of her jeans. Even Frank, the dog who had slept through some drunk breaking Shannon's window after a Cubs loss last October, stirred. He groaned and twisted around until he laid on his back.

With her eyes closed and her face half-buried in her pillow, Shannon's hand searched for the pocket of her jeans.

She pulled out the phone and checked the screen. Its brightness made her squint her one uncovered eye.

It was Layla Pierce—her old friend from the Marines. "Hello?"

"Hey, Shannon," Pierce said. "How're the dunes?"

Shannon balanced her phone on the side of her face. Her free hand went down to rub Frank's ear. "I didn't get to go," she said. "A case came up last night."

"You don't think it'll keep you from coming here, will it?"

"No," Shannon said. "I can pass the case off if it isn't solved by then. I'm working with someone on it."

"That guy you told me about? The cute one?"

Oh, no. Why had she ever told Pierce about Dedrick?

"Since you didn't say anything, I'll take that as a yes," Pierce said.

"Take it as a maybe."

"Well, you won't miss him when you come to Stockholm," she said. "It's a target rich environment. I swear to you, Shannon, every guy here is six feet tall, blond, and beautiful. They love American women. You won't believe it until you see it."

"Mhm."

It was too early to have to endure Pierce's boy craziness. The girl hadn't changed one bit in over a decade. She would've worn Prince out with her sex-drive.

"How's the camping?" Shannon asked.

"Let me ask you something," Pierce said. "What's a six-hour drive from where you are right now?"

"What?" Shannon blinked and rubbed her eyes.

"Where could you be in a six-hour drive from Chicago? Louisville? Green Bay? Cincinnati?"

"Any of those, I think," Shannon said.

"In six hours, I can get you to Copenhagen. That's Denmark, Shannon—another country. In ten hours, I can have you sitting in a beer garden in Hamburg. We can set up a tent right on the Elbe, if that's what you want to do."

Shannon pictured herself sitting on a log, drinking a German hefeweizen, listening to each album from David Bowie's Berlin trilogy. She'd start with Low, then move to Lodger, then Heroes. Maybe it wasn't the order most people would choose, but it was the order she liked.

"The German boys are pretty cute, too," Pierce said.

"What about Michael's job?"

"Ambassador Griggs hosts a gala or dinner or whatever at least twice a week," Piece said. "Michael will definitely be worth his weight in gold. We've been short a sous chef for the last three months. They might throw a parade for him in the kitchen when he arrives."

"And he'll be busy?"

"Yes, very." Pierce laughed. "He might work as much as you do right now."

Shannon paused for a moment. After everything her life had been thus far, working at the US Embassy in Stockholm seemed like an impossible dream. Sometimes she wondered if she were still a little girl hiding in her closet, inventing futures for herself while her drunk father rampaged through the house, hunting for Michael.

"All this talk," Pierce said, "and I'm surprised you haven't double-checked on your own job."

"I'm not worried about myself," Shannon said. "We both know I can handle a security job doing background checks."

"There's the girl I knew," Pierce said. "Cocky as all hell."

Shannon snorted. She grabbed the phone and sat up in her bed, then turned on the bedside lamp.

"So you're sure you'll be here by next week?" Pierce asked. "Because if you aren't, you know I have to move on to another candidate—I've already left your position unfilled way too long as it is."

"I'll be there." Shannon rolled over on her belly and pulled open the bottom drawer of her nightstand. A pair of plane tickets had been tucked in an envelope. "I'm looking at my tickets right now."

"Good," Pierce said. "You know, I can't believe you took on another case this week."

"I know. But I had to take it," Shannon said. "I can't tell you why right now, but I'll talk all about it later."

"Over drinks," Pierce said. "With cute, Swedish boys."

"If they want to hear about murder."

Pierce laughed.

The phone beeped at Shannon. She pulled it away from her face, then looked at the screen. It was Dedrick. He probably had news about the warrant for Colm's townhouse.

"I have to go," she said. "Work's calling me on the other line."

"Okay. Don't miss that flight."

"I won't."

She touched the button on her phone to answer Dedrick's call.

"Please tell me you have something about the warrant," Shannon said.

"No, I just wanted to hear your voice."

"I'd punch you over the phone if I could."

"I know," he said. "But if you did that, you might make me wrinkle the warrant I'm holding right now." There was a brief shuffling of paper in the background. "It authorizes CPD to search for any large sums of money, or signs thereof, at the home of Colm Keane."

"Good," she said. "Meet you at his place?"

"I'm already out the door."

Shannon ended the call. Without looking, she reached down to the waist of her jeans and expected to find her star and gun still there. It wouldn't be the first time she'd collapsed into bed before putting either one in the top drawer of her nightstand. She felt nothing.

Panic fluttered in her chest, until she saw both items neatly placed on top of her nightstand.

"Did you do that?" she said to Frank.

He barely acknowledged her. Not even a flick of his ear. That dog would sleep in her bed all day if it were up to him.

She pulled off the CPD polo she'd worn since yesterday morning. It smelled vaguely of the humid Chicago air and her own sweat. She tossed it in the hamper, changed her bra, then rolled some deodorant on her underarms, and pulled on a new polo.

This one was slate gray instead of dark blue—she had to at least give the illusion she'd showered since last night.

Shannon pulled her hair into a ponytail and held it back with a dark hair tie. She changed out of her jeans and underwear. A pair of dark blue jeans would work— the pair that made her look like she had a butt.

She clipped her gun and star on her hip, then clapped for Frank. "Out of bed, lazybones."

He looked at her from the corners of his eyes. Once again, he tested her.

"Come on, Frank." She grabbed his collar and guided him down.

Out in the hallway, she smelled breakfast. She walked toward the front room.

"Michael?"

"You really shouldn't leave your gun on your hip when you sleep." Michael sat at their small, round table with his laptop in front of him and a half-eaten plate of scrambled eggs and bacon to his left.

"That was you?" she asked.

"Who else?" He stretched in his chair, then turned to look at her. "Frank?"

She shrugged.

"Oh, come on, Shannon. You think I can't take care of you anymore?" He smiled at her like it had been a joke, but she felt the hurt behind his words. "Off to work?" Michael motioned at her star.

"I don't know that I'm ever not working." She brushed past him, into their little kitchenette where a half-emptied pot of coffee stewed on its warmer. "Just came to get a cup before I leave." She pulled a travel mug out of an upper cabinet.

"I can make eggs before you go," he said.

"No, thanks." She poured a splash of creamer into the cup. "I have to get moving. Dedrick is waiting on me."

"It'll only a take a minute." He hopped up from his chair, went to the fridge, and pulled out a carton of eggs. "You gotta eat."

"I've got all I need." She lifted the travel mug at him.

Michael didn't listen. He grabbed a pan from the drying rack next to the sink, cracked two eggs into it, and put it over a burner.

"Give me three minutes." He grinned at her.

She grabbed her coffee and scooted out of the way. Why fight it?

Within seconds of taking her brother's chair at the round kitchenette table, Frank curled up on top of her feet. The militant dog-trainer part of her brain hated that she let him do that, but the rest of her enjoyed feeling his short, bristling hair scratch against the knuckles of her toes.

"Sleep okay last night?" She noticed Michael had Facebook open on his laptop again.

"No," he said. "Did you find anything out?"

"I can't talk about it." She scrolled absent-mindedly through Michael's newsfeed—all the pictures and status updates of his friends. There was a lot of stuff about Colm.

"I know," he said. "I just thought you would."

She stopped at a picture of Colm. He had his tattooed arm hanging over the neck of an absolute knockout—a girl that could have easily graced the front cover of a women's magazine. The picture had been shared by someone named Isabella Arroz. It was three months old.

"Did Colm have a girlfriend?"

"Isabella," Michael said.

"You ever meet her?"

"No, never," he said. "I know he's been with her for a little while, but that's it."

Michael plated the scrambled eggs, grabbed a fork, and brought it all to the table.

"Thanks." Shannon's stomach grumbled. She was hungrier than she realized.

"Colm never was very good with girls." Michael leaned toward the laptop to get a better look at the picture. "But it looks like he made some improvements if he dated her."

"I know," Shannon said through a mouthful of eggs. "She looks like she belongs in one of those murals at a Mexican restaurant."

"She should be standing at the top of an Aztec pyramid with feathers in her hair." Michael spun the laptop back toward him. "Colm knocked it out of the park with her."

Shannon took the last forkful of her eggs. She washed it down with a swallow of coffee. "Thanks for breakfast."

She stood up, kicking Frank off her feet. She gave Michael a kiss on the cheek as she made her way to the door.

"Would you walk Frank again?"

"Sure," Michael said. "It's not like he'd give me a choice anyways."

She grabbed her work bag off the hook next to the door and reached for the knob.

"Hey, Shannon—before you go...."

She stopped and looked to Michael.

"You aren't supposed to talk about it, but I just have to know one thing—and maybe you can't answer yet, but if you can, would you tell me?"

"It depends on what it is."

That seemed to make Michael consider what he was going to say next. "Would you tell me if Colm went back to the mob?"

Oh God, that was the one question she dreaded. What was she supposed to say to that? Right now, it looked like he had. But should she tell Michael that? The answer might pull him to a place they both knew he shouldn't go.

She opened the front door and stepped out into the hallway of their building. "I'll tell you everything I can when I can."

She closed the front door behind her.

What in the hell had she gotten herself into? Maybe she'd figure it out by the time she got back to Colm's house.

CHAPTER 9

"Colm Keane wasn't wanting for locks." Dedrick kicked aside the chips and splinters of what used to be the front door jamb of Colm's house. He wore yesterday's suit—a hint that he hadn't followed his own advice to Shannon. The pair of deputies with them had already fanned out inside the house, leaving the battering ram leaned up against the cream-colored wall in the front entryway.

"The only other time I've ever seen a house with three deadbolts and a keypad lock, I found enough firearms to make my old battalion S2 blush," Shannon said.

"You found a weapons cache in Chicago?"

"No, that was during the cleanup after Fallujah," she said. "The first battle."

Dedrick walked toward a wet bar a few steps into Colm's living room. He approached it, uncorked an empty whiskey bottle, and sniffed it. His head popped back like the vapors had punched him the nose.

"You must've made a pretty picture in camo." He sniffed the bottle again. "I bet you had to knock the other GIs away with the butt of your rifle."

"It wasn't really like that." She leaned up against the wall and watched him work.

He grinned at her, then offered the empty bottle.

"I'll pass, thanks," she said.

He shrugged and sat the bottle down. "Well, I guess this is where all the magic happened," Dedrick said. "Where should we look first? That pile of bottles over there, or the DVD collection?"

Shannon chewed her knuckle and sighed. Colm's house looked like a bachelor pad if she ever saw one— undecorated, unkempt, and a little unsettling.

Which was too bad. The place had good bones. It was an open concept townhouse with high ceilings, hardwood floors, and lots of built-in shelves and cabinets. It looked as if someone had renovated in the last few years. The living and dining room opened into each other, the kitchen was partitioned from the rest of the house, and Shannon guessed the bedrooms and bathroom branched from a hallway off the dining room.

But God, was it ever a mess.

If CPD decided they wanted to test every empty or half-drunk beer bottle Shannon could see in this moment, it'd take them at least six months to get through it all. Bottles piled so high in a trash can in the corner, they tipped over on the floor, and they hid on the built-in shelves between Colm's disheveled collection of DVDs.

The whole house stunk like gym socks and dirty under-wear, too. Shannon wouldn't be surprised if he'd used old laundry to stuff the raggedy, puke-stained couch in the living room—his only piece of furniture, aside from the bar.

She turned over a Chinese takeout box with the toe of her shoe. Thankfully, nothing scurried out from beneath it.

"If you got rid of all the beer bottles, burnt that old couch, and, I dunno, bleached everything else, I bet you'd have an acceptable house for some of Chicago's displaced frat boys," Dedrick said.

"There are plenty up near Wrigley," Shannon said. "I can get the word out."

"If I were one of them, you'd have my full attention."

She rolled her eyes. Lucky for him, he was outside of punching range.

"I want to check out the bedroom," Shannon said. "Experience tells me if we're going to find anything, it'll be there."

She walked past the bar, cutting diagonally across the space that probably would have served as Colm's dining room, if he'd bothered.

The back hallway was almost too dark to see into. Shannon found the light switch. She flicked it on, but nothing happened.

How fitting.

She took her flashlight out of her work bag and turned it on. The hallway was featureless. No pictures, no decorations, no nothing apart from the thermostat on a wall and a couple beer bottles ripening in a corner.

The further she went, the mustier it smelled. There must've been a bathroom behind one of the doors. God help her if they didn't find money, or at least evidence of money, in one of the other rooms.

There was a door at the end of the hall. Shannon turned the brass knob and it drifted open on its own.

On the other side, she saw Colm's room.

It was every bit as messy as the living room, but at least it wasn't worse. The empty beer bottle motif continued here. Half a dozen on top of the dresser, more purposefully stacked into a tight grid in the corner, even one or two at the side of his bed. Maybe he'd drank them in his sleep.

Shannon recalled her father's number one rule for drinking: if you never sober up, you never have a hangover.

She shivered thinking about it. But then, at least Colm had the decency not to inflict himself on an innocent family.

"Looks like our boy was in a hurry to get out of town." Dedrick appeared in the doorway behind her. "That dresser looks worse than the rest of the house."

He was right. A drawer leaned up against the dresser like it had been yanked out and left. Another sat on the floor in front of it. Both held a few items of clothing, but were largely empty. The others were all open to some degree, and looked to be about as empty.

"If he planned on leaving, where was his stuff when he was shot?" Shannon asked.

"Well, kid," Dedrick said, "I'm guessing that, like most other people, he left his bags in his car while he went to the liquor store."

"And I'm guessing you pulled any records we had on him this morning when you put in the warrant request." Shannon took out her pen—one she could part with.

"Ah, dammit," Dedrick said.

"You didn't?"

He turned up his empty hands and grimaced. "I screwed up."

Dedrick didn't say that very often. It wasn't that he was full of himself or couldn't own up to his mistakes—it was that he didn't make many.

"Well, Detective Halman," Shannon said. "Are we getting a little sloppy in our old age?"

He smirked at her. "Let me know when you're done looking through his drawers."

"Oh, gladly."

She used the pen to move aside an old T-shirt in one of the drawers on the ground. She'd be damned if she touched anything in this place, even with her latex gloves on.

Nothing of note beneath the shirt, unless you wanted to see a pair of old jean shorts.

She opened a drawer near the top of the dresser. Underwear. Great. And lots of it still here. If Colm planned on skipping town in the same boxers he left with, anyone who came looking for him would smell him long before they ever saw him.

Shannon sighed. She should've been working her way through some rugged, cute guy's swim trunks right now. They'd both be speckled with dune sand and smelling of Lake Michigan. Instead, she'd been cursed to sort through Colm's nastiness.

Then something beneath the underwear caught her eye. Clear plastic.

She scooped Colm's underwear out of the drawer and tossed it aside.

A plastic baggie. And from inside it, Shannon's own face looked back up at her. It was a picture of her from fourth grade, when she had bangs swooped over her eyebrows and a chunky, awkward little face with a half-smile. She'd stolen that affectation from her brother.

Inside the bag was an entire stack of photos. Shannon hoped they weren't all of her.

"Look at this," she said.

Dedrick popped his head out of Colm's closet. "What?"

Shannon held them up where he could see.

"Is that you?" Dedrick cracked a smile.

"Don't you dare." She narrowed her eyes at him. "I was in fourth grade—I'd like to see what you looked like at that age."

"I was goddamned beautiful," he said. "Of course."

"Of course."

There were enough old photos packed into the baggie that she wasn't sure if she'd split it at the seams on accident. She pulled the two sides of the zipper apart, and the baggie held together. Shannon carefully upended it and let the photos slide out onto Colm's unmade bed.

She fanned them out slowly with the tips of her fingers. A crease or a bent corner might destroy some piece of significant evidence. Or maybe there was a purposeful order to them.

"Just looks like old photos of friends and family," Dedrick said.

Shannon's finger stopped on a picture of herself, Michael, and Colm at Indiana Beach—the old water park in Monticello. They had been in high school. She remembered sneaking into a garage near Boystown before dawn that morning. Colm knew his father had a car stashed there, and he'd hot-wired it. He'd done it without a second thought. Just like that, they were off.

"How old were you there?" Dedrick asked. "Fifteen? Sixteen?"

"Fourteen," she said. "Colm tried to kiss me that day."

"Yeah? What happened?"

"Michael saw us and punched him in the gut just a half-second before we actually did it."

Dedrick shook his head.

"What?" she said.

"You don't kiss your best friend's little sister," he said. "That's a breach in the guy code. A pretty serious one."

She laughed to herself and put the picture back in its place on the bed. "Makes perfect sense Colm did it, then," she said. "He did what he wanted, when he wanted."

"If he had a wild streak, I can see why you fell for him. You like bad boys."

"Oh? Do I?"

Dedrick was one smartass comment away from getting his armed punched.

"Sure," he said. "And that's good news for me—I'm a good guy."

She decked him just above the elbow.

"Detective Rourke?" An officer called for her from the hallway. "Detective Rourke, are you back here?"

"At the end of the hall," she called back. "Detective Halman and I are in the master bedroom."

She expected a smart comment from Dedrick, but he feigned innocence and held up his hands.

"Detectives." The officer poked his head into the room. It was Dan Coughlin. His head was shaved into a mirror shine and it caught the paltry light in Colm's bedroom. "I think you should see something out here."

They followed Coughlin back into Colm's living room. Near a pile of opened DVD cases, a rectangular safe no larger than a briefcase waited on the floor in front of the TV.

"That's new," Dedrick said. "Where'd you find it?"

"In that vent." Coughlin pointed to a square hole in the wall behind one of the upper shelves. "I've seen dope dealers hide money and whatever else inside DVD cases before, so I took it upon myself to go through all these DVDs on the shelf." He motioned toward the pile of opened DVD cases on the ground. "That's when I noticed the vent behind them."

A silver thread had been tied around the handle of the case. It was around six feet long. Shannon dropped to her knees, then picked the wire up. It was braided steel, probably about a sixteenth or an eighth of an inch thick.

"Picture wire," she said.

Coughlin nodded.

"What made you decide to check that vent?" she asked.

"My dad was an HVAC man—used to run the duct work in houses under construction. I helped him a couple summers when I was in college," he said. "Soon as I looked at that vent, I noticed part of the duct was missing. I took the grate off and I saw that wire wrapped around a roofing nail on the inside of the wall. I pulled it out, and sure enough...." He motioned toward the safe.

"Pretty good hiding spot," Dedrick said.

"Can we get this open?" Shannon ran her thumbs along the seam of the case's two halves.

"I've got a pry bar in the back of my cruiser," Coughlin said, "if you two feel like we have PC for this."

"It's a locked case hidden in the walls of the home of a man with Irish Mob connections," Dedrick said. "I think it'd be easy to argue that the money we're looking for could be in there."

"We're covered under our warrant," Shannon said. "Go get the pry bar."

Officer Coughlin ran out the front door in a heartbeat. Not thirty seconds later, he came back with the pry bar in his hand—a flattened piece of black steel, scratched up from use.

He looked at the small safe and licked his lips. Easy pickings for a man his size.

Shannon motioned for him to wait a moment. She pulled out her cell phone and snapped a picture of the safe. Who knew what it'd look like when the officer finished opening it?

"Detective?" He offered the pry bar to Shannon.

"Oh, no." She held up her hands. "You found the box, you do the honors."

"I was hoping you'd say that." Coughlin looked like a kid scouting porches for pumpkins a few days after Halloween.

Using his foot, he pushed the safe up against the wall beneath the front window. Then, with one motion, he reared back and jammed the straight end of the pry bar between the upper and lower halves.

He had the pry bar stuck in the safe like it was a lollypop stick.

"You need a little help?" Dedrick said.

"I've got it, Detective." Coughlin looked over his shoulder. "But you might want to take a step or two back."

Shannon and Dedrick exchanged a puzzled look. He stepped back, then he pulled her with him.

"Here we go." Coughlin grabbed the pry bar. He jiggled it a little bit, seeing if he could separate it from the case, or if the two were as stuck together as they looked.

The safe moved with the pry bar. They were stuck together. No question.

He hoisted the entire thing over his head like a sledge-hammer. It stayed aloft, and for a split second, Shannon thought the case would go flying off the end of the pry bar. But they stayed together—up until the moment he smashed it into the ground. There was a crack like he'd split the sub-floor open, but the noise came from the safe. He bashed it down three, maybe four more times before it split open like a walnut.

The damn safe was empty.

Officer Coughlin stood over it, panting and holding the pry bar like a club.

"Nice job, Lunk." Dedrick put a hand on his shoulder. "If we ever need someone to club a dinosaur, we know who to call."

"Thanks," Coughlin said.

Shannon stepped up to one half of the case and turned it over. It was only naked, gunmetal-gray plastic on the inside. Not a single cent. Not even a bank slip.

She put her nose toward it, and sniffed the inside of the case. "It smells like money."

"That's a start, but we have to find better evidence," Dedrick said. "We keep looking here, and I know something else is gonna turn up."

CHAPTER 10

"Four hours of raking through Colm's house, and the only thing we turned up was an empty safe." Shannon wiped a bit of the June humidity off her forehead. She sat in front of Colm's house with Dedrick, her legs hanging off of the open back of her Jeep.

"That's not true," Dedrick said. "We found a half-gram of stale weed mashed into the carpet, a prescription pill bottle with someone else's name on it, and some dirty anime DVDs stashed under Colm's mattress."

"Not even a checkbook to be found," Shannon said.

"I don't think that kid used a bank." Dedrick leaned on the hood of his black Impala, his jacket off and arms crossed. He stared at Colm's front door as if he could will some new piece of evidence to materialize. "We should've known from the start there wouldn't be any money in that place," he said. "Colm's wallet was close to exploding from all the money he had stuffed in it, and his room was ransacked like he wanted to get out in a hurry. Why would he have left a single dollar behind? Hell, for all we know, every dime he had was in his wallet when we found him."

Shannon looked over some of the random notes she'd scratched down in her notebook. *No sign of forced entry.* "That's the thing I don't understand," she said. "The clerk at the liquor store didn't mention anything about Colm looking rushed. So why was his room such a mess?"

"Maybe Colm *was* in a hurry and the clerk didn't notice. Witnesses miss details all the time," Dedrick said. "Could be he had an itch for a drink, so he played it cool for a minute. It isn't a stretch to think the kid needed booze. We're talking about somebody who probably did a shot of Rumple Minze every morning instead of brushing his teeth."

She sighed. Of all the people to get murdered in Chicago, why did it have to be Colm? And why right now?

"Sorry," Dedrick said. "I crossed a line."

"It's all right." She gave him a weak smile. "Did you sleep last night?"

"Oh, yeah." A corner of his mouth lifted. "I slept like a baby."

"For how long?"

"I caught an hour or two in one of the interrogation rooms."

"Thought so," Shannon said.

"I'm still fit for duty."

"Not in the same suit you wore yesterday."

He flashed the brightest smile he could manage at her. "Well, Detective Rourke, I never knew you cared."

She laughed. "Don't take it the wrong way—the only reason I mention it is because the smell's getting to me."

"It's more of a gentle musk." Dedrick raised his arms and sniffed his own armpits. "Like a summer breeze through a garbage dump."

Shannon threw her head back and laughed a little louder than she'd intended.

When she regained herself, she found her eyes drawn to Dedrick's. She lingered a little too long on him for her own comfort. Shannon couldn't help it. She liked being around Dedrick, liked punching his arm, and rolling her eyes at him. It'd been a long time since she'd come in contact with someone like that—not since AJ.

She forced her eyes down to her notes again.

"You know," she said, "money or not, Colm was into something. The money left in his wallet, the number of times he'd been shot, all those cigarettes indicating someone may have waited for him…. If there wasn't ever any money to find, there's still someone out there who wanted him dead."

"This wasn't a mugging gone bad," Dedrick said. "The only question is if we'll ever see anything turn up."

"If we stay on the case, we will."

"If *I* stay on the case, you mean. You're leaving for Stockholm in a couple days, right?"

"You know what I meant."

Dedrick stood up, rubbed his face, then yawned. "Who do you think our guy pissed off?"

Shannon shrugged. "If he had money, I know he didn't get it by legitimate means. Colm wasn't the kind of guy who went out and hustled his way to the top. He'd take the easiest way to whatever he wanted."

"All right." Dedrick rubbed his eyes. "So, an old running partner. Maybe somebody he did some dirt with."

"Could be." Shannon kicked her legs back and forth off the edge of her Jeep's tailgate. She scribbled Dedrick's theory down.

"Know anyone we can talk to about that?"

"You think I know someone?" She raised an eyebrow at him.

"Well, you were friends with Colm Keane, right? He knew people. Hell, his dad is somebody."

"You think CPD would let me in if I knew someone like that?"

"Sure they would," he said. "You bring some goons in to break some knees or strong-arm the right person, and you're working in Violent Crimes."

She rolled her eyes at him.

"All right, maybe not," he said. "Could be that he took the money from someone he shouldn't have taken it from."

"I wouldn't put it past him," Shannon said. "Colm wasn't necessarily a stickup kid, but he was hot-headed enough to have that in him."

"You think his dad would retaliate against whoever killed him?"

"I don't know," she said. "It probably depends on who he ripped off. Last I knew, Colm and his father weren't really on the best terms. I don't think that's changed."

"Still," Dedrick said, "Colm's his son. And a guy as connected as Ewan Keane doesn't stay in this game as long as he has by sitting on his hands."

"We can check that angle tomorrow," she said. "Ewan keeps an office in Boystown."

"Think he'd talk to the police?"

"Probably not," Shannon said. "But he'd talk to the daughter of his old friend, Tommy Rourke."

Dedrick looked at her sideways. "I thought you said you didn't have connections like that."

"I don't," she said. "But my father did. As a rule, I try not to follow in his footsteps."

He nodded and yawned.

"There's another thing I'd like to follow up on," Shannon said. "Turns out Colm had a girlfriend."

"What makes you think that?"

"Facebook."

"Facebook." Dedrick snorted. "God help the twenty-first century cop who can't stand Facebook."

"Well, you'll be glad to know she has her account set to private. Other than her name, I don't know much about her."

"Solid lead, Detective." Dedrick straightened out and popped his back. He desperately tried to stay awake now. "What's her name?"

"Isabella Arroz." Shannon circled Isabella's name on her notes.

"And what makes you think she was his girlfriend?"

"Michael said so. I also saw a couple pictures of them. I guess I assume they're together by the way he held her in them—the way the two of them looked together. I can't explain it."

"Sounds like women's intuiti—"

"Don't you dare finish that word," Shannon said. "If I hear another person in this department put another smart observation under the category of 'women's intuition' again, I'm going to scream."

Dedrick tried to say something smart back to her, but his yawn washed it out of his mouth.

"You're a hypocrite, by the way," Shannon said. "You were on me about going to get some sleep this morning, and you can barely stand up straight."

He grinned at her, his eyes fighting to stay halfway opened.

"Go home," she said. "I'll take it from here."

"What?" he said. "You're going to solve this thing without me? Who'll make all the wisecracks—and don't say you will, Shannon. We both know you can't hold a candle to me."

"I would never presume to be better than the master," she said. "But I don't think I'll have to be. I'm on my way to Colm's wake."

"Irish wake." He chuckled. "I'm better off staying away. Tired as I am, I'll pass out after I take my first swallow of beer."

"What a shame," she said.

He smiled at her. "Looks like you'll have to trick me into getting drinks with you some other time."

She felt her cheeks blush at the idea. Hopping down from the back of her Jeep, she turned as quick as she could and slammed the tailgate shut. She didn't want him to catch her.

"Darn." She held her voice flat. "Almost had you."

"Some other day, Shannon." His car door whined open. "I know you can't have fun without me, so I'll just leave it at that."

He closed it behind him and started the engine.

She waved at him, hoping her cheeks weren't flushed any longer. He waved back, and her heart fluttered in her chest like a little girl seeing her crush across the class room.

To think she'd been a United States Marine once.

If only everything were as simple as carting supplies back and forth across Iraq.

CHAPTER 11

After Dedrick drove off, Shannon went back up to Colm's porch. She caught Officer Coughlin, Mr. Handy-With-A-Pry-Bar, on his way out.

"Find anything else?" Shannon asked.

"Just a whole mess of empty booze bottles and some dirty socks." Officer Coughlin marked the front door with crime scene tape. "Looks like our guy hardly kept anything personal."

"No laptop?"

"One that doesn't work," he said.

"Did you bag it?"

Coughlin nodded.

"How about a cell phone?" she asked.

"We found a couple burners around the house, but the ones that ain't password protected are busted."

Shannon sighed.

"Detective, I wish we would've found something more," Coughlin said. "I wish we would've found something that kept me from searching his bathroom."

"And we're sure we had someone watching the house last night?"

"That's right," Coughlin said. "I relieved Officer Knox this morning. Parked my cruiser right where it is now—" he pointed at it across the street "—and never took my eyes off this place until you and Detective Halman came by."

Shannon frowned at the house. There had to be something else there. Locard's Exchange Principle had never failed her in the past.

"Good work, Coughlin." She clapped his shoulder. "I appreciate you being here today."

Coughlin picked up his roll of yellow tape, then gave her a nod. She watched him get in his cruiser and drive away.

When the car was out of sight, she walked south down Albany Street.

No signs of forced entry at Colm's house, and anything that may have given the police some clue as to what Colm had been into—who he spoke with and why he was halfway across town at that liquor store on Ashland—had been mysteriously absent.

Shannon stepped off the curb at North Avenue. Across the street, she saw McCullough's Pub. Convenient that Colm's wake would be held so close to his house, and at a bar he had apparently been to.

After a short walk down the road, Shannon opened the front door of the pub. It was just after 8 o'clock.

McCullough's Pub was small and dark. She could probably walk from one wall to another in ten steps if it weren't for the mess of tables and chairs cluttering the place. There were so many brewery logos, neon signs, and pictures of half-naked women on the walls, she wondered if they held the roof up. In the little blank spaces between them, she saw hints of faux wood paneling.

One wall had a large picture of Colm's face—taken straight from this Facebook profile photo. Bunches and bunches of flowers surrounded it. So many that they almost covered up the stink of stale beer and piss that Shannon assumed was the natural aroma of McCullough's.

It came as no surprise that Colm had liked the place.

Michael had already claimed a spot in a booth directly across from the front door. Two of his high school friends, Henry Jackson and Ryan Tooley, yelled at him from across the table in a way that only thoroughly drunk men could.

The wake had only started an hour ago. It looked to be a long night.

Her brother spotted her. He waved her over. She made her way through the tables and chairs toward him.

"I'm surprised someone got a wake together already." She scooted in next to Michael on the wooden bench.

"Word gets around," Michael said.

"How'd they get a place so quickly?"

"You didn't know Colm's dad was part-owner of McCullough's?"

She blinked at her brother. "Should I have?"

"Oh, that's right—he bought into it when you were out in Iraq. Colm wouldn't shut up about it. Said he was going to drink the place dry the first weekend after all the papers had been signed."

If his house were anything to go by, he probably could have done it, too.

"You were in Iraq, Shannon?" Ryan Tooley looked at her with wide eyes. "What branch?"

"Marines," she said. "I did a tour in 2006."

"Oh, yeah?" Ryan asked. "My cousin was there with the Army—you know a guy by the name of Greg Bandert?"

Shannon shook her head. "There were a lot of people there."

"They keep you in the back?" Henry Jackson's mouth was half-buried in his glass. He took a drink and swallowed. "You know, since you're a woman and all?"

"I drove a truck, if that's what you're asking." She could already see this conversation heading in a direction she didn't like.

"Oh, so you didn't ever shoot nobody."

She kept her mouth shut and looked at him.

"Yeah, she left that to the men." Ryan flexed and nearly choked himself from laughing. He acted as if he'd been in the war. In reality, the closest he came to being in the service was probably if he drove past a recruiting center nestled in a strip mall somewhere. "Bet you never even fired a rifle, did you?"

Shannon squeezed her fist. It wouldn't be right to kick the hell out of one of them. They were morons, sure, but they were harmless.

Shannon tried to talk over their cackling.

She heard her Drill Instructor's voice bellowing in her head: *"Every Marine is a rifleman! I don't care If you're greasing wheel bearings or making lunch for the SEALs. If any of you recruits are deemed worthy to become part of the United States Marine Corps, you'll be able to shoot the ass off a fly at a hundred yards."*

"Every Marine is a riflem—"

Michael cut her off when he slammed his glass of cranberry juice on the table.

The laughing quit.

Michael looked from Ryan to Henry and back. "I respect the hell out of Shannon for doing what she did over there."

It didn't feel like praise for his sister. The way he said it made it feel more like a threat against the two men sitting across the table from him: respect my family, or I'll knock your teeth down your throat.

Ryan looked at Shannon in silence for a moment. Henry took another sip of his beer.

"Sorry, Shannon," Ryan said. "I didn't mean nothing by it—just kidding you a little bit."

"It's fine," she said. "I wasn't offended."

She wished Michael wouldn't have made a big deal about it. He didn't have to protect her anymore.

"I'm gonna go walk and talk," Michael said. He nearly pushed Shannon out of the booth, but she found her feet quick enough to get up and let him pass.

She'd have to keep an eye on him tonight. Being exposed to Ryan and Henry were pretty low on the list of bad things that could happen to Michael here. There'd be other people who showed up later. People she should be concerned about.

"I'm gonna step out for a cig," Ryan said. "Henry, you coming with?"

He slammed his glass down and followed Ryan out of the booth.

Shannon slid back in. She took out her phone and reflexively opened Facebook. What the hell was she doing here? Keeping Michael out of trouble? Working? Neither? Maybe it'd be better if she left now.

Shannon slid her phone back in her pocket and got up from the booth.

"I didn't think you'd be leaving so early, Shannon."

Ewan Keane, Colm's father, stood in front of her.

If she didn't know better, she wouldn't think he was a captain in the Irish Mob. He wasn't some blowhard pumped full of bravado and booze. He had a firm, intelligent way of speaking—one that made it easy to fall under his spell. His face was kind and there was a disarming way about him. Ewan Keane looked like the sort of man you hoped your widowed mother would bring to Thanksgiving—someone you assumed would treat her right just by looking at him.

He wore a fitted black suit to his son's wake. His face was cleanly shaved, and his white hair freshly cut and parted. His cologne smelled like roasted pine.

Shannon had to admit, he looked good.

Ewan motioned toward the empty bench across the table from her. "Would it be a bother if I took a seat?"

"You own the place." She slid back into her spot on the bench. Maybe she'd get to ask a couple questions.

"That I do," he smiled at her as he eased into the seat. "And I must admit, I'm a little surprised to see you and your brother here, Shannon."

"We were Colm's friends."

"Of course you were." He folded his hands on the table. "Would you care for a drink? I'm buying."

She looked over the tops of all the heads and between all the people mingling around the tables and chairs in the middle of the bar. No sign of Michael. She wouldn't be able to escape that easily.

"You've been to enough of these to know it's rude to turn down a drink from a family member of the deceased," Ewan said.

"I'll have a rum and Coke," she said without thinking.

Ewan raised a finger. A waitress was over before Shannon could change her mind.

"My guest would like a rum and Coke," he said. "Give her something from my private collection."

"Which rum exactly, sir?" the waitress asked.

Ewan looked Shannon over. "How about the Santa Teresa? There should be a bottle in the basement near the walk-in."

"And for you, sir?"

"A glass of Laphroaig 18."

The waitress was off. She cut through the crowd of people as if she were on a life or death mission.

"I think she'll be one my premiere staff members," Ewan said, "but she needs to learn the drink list a little better."

Shannon gave him a tight-lipped smile. "Mr. Keane, may I ask what you want from me?"

He leaned back in the booth and interlocked his fingers in his lap. "That's funny. You sounded like your father just now."

Shannon's skin crawled. "I'll try to watch what I say next time."

"I know you probably weren't his biggest fan," Ewan said. "That was obvious when you didn't show up to his funeral—but you might be surprised to learn he had a few redeeming qualities."

"I would be very surprised," she said.

Ewan laughed. "You've got his relentlessness, you know. He passed you his knack for cutting through all the mess and getting to the point. I think that was the trait I valued in him the most."

"Then you wouldn't mind if I asked you about Colm's girlfriend," Shannon said.

"I wouldn't mind at all. But I don't think I'd be able to tell you much."

"Why not?"

"My son rarely clued me in to his personal life," Ewan said. "Until you informed me, I had no idea he was seeing anyone."

"I find that hard to believe."

"You do?"

"I do," she said. "You knew about his death quickly enough to throw this wake together and get all of these people here, but you expect me to believe he was able to keep his girlfriend a secret from you?"

Ewan laughed.

"What?" she asked.

"If you think I had spies watching my son or some other way of keeping tabs on him, you should think again," he said. "It was your brother, Michael. He called me about Colm's death last night."

There was nothing to like about Michael talking to Ewan. Shannon felt her nerves bundle up in her stomach.

The waitress popped up at the end of the both again, two drinks on a round tray. One was Ewan's Scotch. The other had a lime slice hanging off the rim of the glass. She passed it to Shannon.

"To Colm." Ewan lifted his glass.

Shannon did the same. They both took a sip.

Think what she may about Ewan Keane—the man knew how to stock a bar. The rum in her drink was sweet with a little bite, but not overpowering—just enough flavor to tell her it was in the glass.

Ewan held his glass at eye-level and studied his drink. He looked pleased with himself. "I know what you must think," he said. "But I didn't come sit with you so I could work you over. I'm sure I've got a reputation at CPD, if not with you personally, Shannon, and I want to lay any fears you have to rest."

"What would I be afraid of?"

He shot her a polite smile. "I can pretend you're duller than we both know you are, if that's what would please you. But I thought you'd find that insulting."

He waved his glass at the rest of the bar. The ice cubes clinked inside of it. "All these people here tonight to celebrate Colm, and not one of them knows you or your family like I do. Even the people here with connections—they don't understand your brother the same as me."

She tried not to clench her jaw at the mention of Michael.

"I don't mean that as a threat or an allusion," Ewan said. "I meant that exactly as it came out. I respect you and your wishes to stay apart from the rest of us. I respect your brother's new life. I understand why he left us, and I wish the best to both of you. And out of that same respect, I'm willing to speak with you, as it concerns Colm."

As if it came from thin air, he had a business card under his fingers. He slid it toward her.

Shannon took it. Ewan's name and address were printed neatly on it.

Was he telling the truth? Would Ewan Keane, a man with more reasons than not to avoid the Chicago PD, willingly help her? She studied his eyes for a moment. They nestled inside the rugose skin on his face, cool and light blue—unflinching.

"Why?" It was all she could think to ask.

"I have associates who would rather see that Michael didn't get involved. So, I'd like to provide you with any information I have."

"Is that because one of them killed your son?"

"No," Ewan said sharply. "I wouldn't let them touch a hair on Colm's head—but you just demonstrated why we'd rather not have Michael insert himself into this. Anyone looking at this from the outside would be suspicious of them—just as you are." He took a drink of Scotch. "If Michael's suspicions of my friends gets the better of him, even I can't stop them from retaliating against him.

"I'm sure that you know how persistent he can be when he's made his mind up about something, and I know you don't want to see your brother hurt," Ewan said. "Trust me. No part of me wants that either."

She laughed. "That's the problem, I can't trust you."

Ewan took the last sip of his Scotch. He moved his closed lips up and down, chewing the alcohol, then swallowed. He tilted the glass on the table and rotated it on its bottom edge, watching it focus and refract the dim lights in the bar.

"One day, I hope you come to the realization that I've always been on your family's side, Shannon. Since the moment I met your father, and every moment thereafter."

Ewan excused himself from the table, adjusted the knot on his tie, then turned around. Someone walked in the door and called his name. He left Shannon to go say hello.

She scanned the room for Michael. He sat on a bar stool, leaning over a glass of cranberry juice by himself. She had no idea what she'd say to him.

CHAPTER 12

"You know, the last time I came to this bar, Colm beat the hell out of some guy in that corner over there." Michael pointed at a corner where a pair of digital dartboards mumbled to themselves. "The dartboards weren't here back then."

Shannon pushed her empty glass away. She signaled the bartender for another. "Why'd he do it?"

"Told me he didn't like the guy." Michael traced the rim of his glass with his finger. "I never could get a straight answer out of him about it. For all I know, he did it for fun."

Shannon looked over her shoulder at the giant picture of Colm. "He was a real prick, wasn't he?" The bartender sat a fresh rum and Coke in front of Shannon. "But here all these people are, talking about him, remembering him. Do you think any of them really knew who he was?"

"Probably not." Michael shrugged. "I'm not sure I did."

"I should talk to some of them," she said. "That would be the responsible thing to do."

"Then why don't you?"

"Half of them would walk away from me, and the other half wouldn't be able to tell me anything useful." She pulled Ewan's business card out of her pocket and passed it to Michael. "Anyway, I've got the cooperation of the one person here who's supposed to know Colm best."

He looked at it and laughed. "Yeah. Okay."

She put it back.

"Did you need Ewan's business card to find him?"

"No," she said. "But it's nice to know he's serious about talking to CPD. I might get lucky and catch him with a couple kilos of coke on his desk."

She waited for Michael to laugh, but he all he did was stare at the last few drops of cranberry juice in his glass.

"Watch yourself around him," Michael said. "I've seen that man do things to people you wouldn't begin to believe."

"He wouldn't touch me." To her right, she heard Ewan's laughter roar above the din of loud conversation in the bar. He slapped somebody on the back and flagged down his favorite waitress for another drink.

"That's the exact attitude Ewan preys on."

And how would Michael know, exactly? What had he done that allowed him to see that side of Ewan?

She picked at the edge of her napkin. There were a hundred questions she wanted to ask her brother, and all of them were better left unsaid.

"What is it?" Michael asked.

"Nothing. It doesn't matter."

"Don't hold secrets from me."

Funny he'd say that.

"You don't want to hear it."

"Yes, I do."

She narrowed her eyes at him. "I think it's strange that I can sit right here on this stool next to you. I can reach out and touch your arm, I can hug you, I can toss your glass off the bar, but sometimes I feel like you're so far away, I can't see who you are."

He sighed and leaned away from her. His eyes took a pass around the bar like he waited for someone to jump out of the crowd and stab him.

"Michael, I just had a known mobster come over and practically beg me to make sure you stayed out of anything to do with Colm."

He perfectly executed his cocky half-smile as he fished a piece of ice out of his glass and popped it in his mouth. "Yeah?"

"Why's that funny to you?" she asked.

He shrugged.

"When I left for the Marines, you promised me you wouldn't do what Tommy did," she said. "But when I came back to Chicago three years later, all I heard from our old friends was how you're lying in a halfway house somewhere with a needle in your arm—no explanation of how you got that way, or why you did it.

"That was ten years ago, Michael. It's been five years since you got clean for good and I still don't have an explanation." She laid her hand on his wrist. "Do you understand what that does to me?"

He pulled his arm away. His eyes locked on Ewan Keane yukking it up with his buddies at one of the tables near the edge of Colm's mess of flowers. "I won't tell you because I'm not proud of anything I did while you were gone," Michael said. "Leave it at that."

"I can't," she said. "You know I can't."

Michael turned to her, ready to say something else when a hand dropped to his shoulder. It was Ryan's. Henry stood just behind him.

"Mikey, we're going to Wrigleyville." Spit leapt from Ryan's mouth with every syllable. He swayed like his bones were made out of jelly. "You're coming with us."

"I appreciate the offer," Michael said, "but I'm staying here."

"What?" Ryan looked at him like he'd just confessed to shooting his dog. "No, you gotta come with us. We're gonna have fun."

"No, I don't."

"You're not planning on staying here with them all night, are you?" Ryan swayed to his left, then regained his balance at the last second. "You and Colm weren't even friends like that, were you? Hadn't you dropped off the face of the Earth the last few years?"

"We were friends," Michael said. "And I'm not going to the bars with you."

"It's Wrigleyville, man! Don't you live down the street?"

Michael jumped off his stool. "I said I'm not going."

Ryan put his hands up and slowly stepped back. "I'm not trying to start nothing with you, Mikey—just thought you looked like a special sort of miserable since you been sober so long." He laughed. "Don't want you to blow your brains out like your old man."

That was the wrong thing to say.

Michael swung on him faster than Shannon could react. His fist connected to Ryan's chin in a split second, and Ryan stumbled back into a table, spilling drinks and tripping over himself as he tried to regain his composure.

Shannon wrapped her arms around her brother. "Stop it!" she yelled.

Michael didn't try to get away from her.

Nobody in the bar seemed upset that he'd knocked Ryan out. There were whistles and laughing while Henry ran over to pull Ryan off the ground.

"Now it's a wake!" someone yelled.

Shannon turned Michael toward the door, and walked out with her arms around him.

"You can let me go now," Michael said as soon as they were outside.

The words came out a little cooler than Shannon expected. She dropped her arms from her brother and took a couple steps away from him.

It had been years since she'd seen this side of him. Part of her hoped he'd left his anger behind him, but that was naive, wasn't it? You couldn't shrug off the things he went through. You couldn't wake up one day and decide to forget nearly twenty years of your life.

Underneath that cool exterior, he was a powder keg. He'd been that way ever since she could remember.

She watched him pull a steel cigarette case out of his front pocket. It looked familiar.

"Wasn't that Tommy's?" she asked.

Michael flicked it open with his thumb. The top reflected the green light from the McCullough's sign, revealing all the delicate, complex lines etched into it. For some reason, the design on her father's cigarette case always reminded her of wind.

He laid a cigarette on his bottom lip.

"It is, isn't it?" She swiped for the case, but Michael was faster.

It clicked shut in his hand. He slid it back into his front pocket, then produced a lighter.

"Why do you have that?"

"It was Dad's." The cigarette bounced on his lips. He held his hand up to it, flicked the lighter on, then took his first puff. "Why wouldn't I?"

"Because it was his," she said. "Why would you want to keep anything that belonged to him?"

"Ewan gave it to me." He shrugged. "Didn't seem right not to take it."

"That doesn't mean you have to use it," she said. "That doesn't even mean you have to keep it. You could do what everyone does when they get something meaningful they don't really want—just put it in a closet somewhere and forget about it."

"I'm not everyone else." He watched a moth dance around the neon lights of the sign.

There was no getting to him when he didn't want to talk about something. There was especially no debating decisions he made.

"Find anything new about Colm?" he asked.

"You shouldn't ask me that."

"Why not?"

"Because I've been drinking." She pinched the bridge of her nose. Two rum and Cokes already. Work would be miserable tomorrow. "The investigation isn't going well."

Michael sighed. The cigarette's cherry brightened under his breath. "How about an information exchange?" he asked.

"You can't be serious."

"Sure I am," he said. "I'll tell you something I know about Colm, you tell me something you know."

Shannon looked him over. He *was* serious, wasn't he?
"Why not simply tell me what you know?" she asked.
"Wouldn't be fair."
What in the hell was this to him? A game?
Shannon ran her fingers over her hair. She didn't have anything to lose. If she told Michael what she knew, it wasn't like her brother would blab to anyone. He knew how to keep his mouth shut, if he knew how to do anything. Then again, she didn't exactly have anything Earth-shattering on Colm.
"Okay," she said. "But whatever I tell you stays with you."
"I expect the same."
"I can't make that promise," Shannon said. "If you know something specific and you tell me, I'm bound by my job to share it with the court, should things come to that."
He flicked the cigarette. It shook off its own ash. "Okay."
This would turn out to be a horrible idea.
"Fine," she said. "You first."
Michael put the cigarette to his mouth and drew deep, burning off a half-inch in one breath. He exhaled. The smoke billowed out from his mouth, obscuring his face for a moment. "When I told you I hadn't talked to Colm, I lied," he said. "He and I talked every day for the last six months."
Shannon's eyes widened. "When? I never saw you on the phone."
"With as much as you work, that wasn't hard to pull off."
"Why didn't you tell me?"

"Because of what he and I talked about."

Oh no. The color drained from her face. Bad idea after bad idea raced through her head. When they were all kids, Colm and Michael sometimes got into a self-destructive feedback loop together. One would dare the second to break a window. The second would do it and dare the first to steal a six-pack from a convenience store. It went on and on like that, before someone would usually back down, but not before a number of things had been stolen or broken into.

But they weren't teenage delinquents anymore. They were men with terrible impulses. God only knows what ideas Colm had put in his head these last few months.

"It isn't what you might think," Michael said. "Colm was a different person. Still an asshole, but different."

"Then what was it?" she said.

He shook his head and puffed the cigarette. "I told you something, now you tell me something."

"What do you want to know?" She'd already told him the investigation wasn't going well. What else could she offer?

"I didn't ask you that before I told you something," Michael said.

Where to start? She wished she had her notes with her, but she'd left her work bag in her Jeep, which was currently parked in front of Colm's house.

"I think Colm was an alcoholic," she said. "There were empty bottles everywhere in his house."

"I knew that."

"Because you talked to him?"

"Sort of."

"Can you give me a straight answer on anything?"

"Look, Shannon, there are things I *want* to tell you, and things I *can* tell you. There's only a little overlap between the two."

"And how much of it will help me figure out who killed Colm?"

He stepped on a June bug sojourning near a piece of gum on the sidewalk. 1"I don't know," he said. "That's why I need to know what you've found. I think we both have a couple pieces of the same puzzle, and no box to look at."

Her brother was tight-lipped as ever, and maybe a little more cryptic—but she was desperate for information.

"We think Colm may have come into some money," she said. "I'm looking at that as a possible motive."

"What makes you say that?" Michael didn't look surprised in the least. Then again, he never did.

"Something a neighbor told me tipped me off initially," she said. "Based on that, Dedrick Halman and I had a warrant issued to search Colm's house, but the only significant thing we found was an empty lockbox hidden in the wall."

Michael pursed his lips. She recognized the expression. It was the same one he used when he looked over the menu at Murphy's Bleachers—he had a decision to make.

"Tell me he wasn't involved with Ewan's business again," she said.

"I don't think he was," Michael said. "His girlfriend, Isabella, is pregnant. He wanted to change his life around for her, and I know working for his dad, above anything else, went against that."

"Am I right about the money?" Shannon asked.

"I don't know. But it explains some things."

"Like what?"

"He was worried about Isabella. She was on him about something," Michael said. "A couple weeks ago, I think it stopped."

"What gave you that impression?"

Michael tossed the cigarette into the street. "He seemed happier, like he wasn't worried about anything anymore."

"And you don't know why?"

"No," Michael said. "He said it was better for me if I didn't know."

It didn't take a genius to figure out the most-likely answer.

"The money," she said. "That's when he came into the money."

"I know he didn't get it from working with anyone in the family business," Michael said.

"How can you be sure?"

Michael opened his mouth, then he hesitated.

"What is it?"

He went for the cigarette case in his pocket again. Shannon grabbed his wrist and held it there against his hip. She had it so tight, she felt every nervous twitch of his muscles as if they were her own.

"If you don't tell me whatever it is you're holding back, I may not be able to find out who's responsible for what happened to Colm. I know you don't want that."

Michael's eyes stopped on something inside the bar, just over her shoulder. He sighed and looked at her hand on his. Who knew what went through his head?

"He and I had been going to twelve-step together," Michael said. "I was his sponsor."

She let go of her brother.

"I know he didn't go to work for Ewan. He told me the work Ewan gave him drove him to drink," Michael said.

"Why didn't you say something?"

He pulled out the cigarette case, opened it, and took out another. "He told me all that in trust, Shannon," he said. "Everything Colm said in the meetings, everything he said to me—I'm not supposed to let it out."

She balled up her fist. She had to stop herself from yelling at him. She knew how seriously Michael treated his twelve-step program, and she was glad for it. Better that than have him sticking a needle in his arm. But this was a murder investigation, for God's sake.

"If you know anything else about Colm that you think has any bearing on this case, I need you to tell me," she said. "Like you said, I need your puzzle pieces."

"We traded stories about the things we'd do to get high, or in his case, get a drink." Michael lit his cigarette. "We called each other when we had compulsions to do it again. We talked about strategies for staying sober and the things that made us use—that's how I know he wasn't involved with Ewan's business."

"If you saw the inside of his house, you might change your mind about that." She looked over her shoulder at all the people drinking to Colm's memory.

"Colm was only a few months into the program," Michael said. "I'm sure he had setbacks—but I know his desire to recover was real."

"If he had setbacks, I'm having a hard time believing he never worked for his father."

Ewan stood at the corner of the bar, laughing and back-slapping with a couple other men—people Shannon didn't recognize. His eyes brushed over her, then returned to his Scotch.

"So, what, you think Ewan got his own son killed?"

"Maybe," Shannon said.

Her brother stamped out his cigarette.

"Hello, Michael," someone said from their right.

Shannon turned and saw Elizabeth Keane—Ewan's daughter, Colm's sister, and Michael's ex-fiancée—a few steps off.

Robbie Simmons stood next to her.

CHAPTER 13

"Elizabeth." If Michael had a cigarette in his mouth, it would've burned a gash into his shirt as it fell out and slid down. "What are you doing here?"

"It's my brother's wake." Elizabeth smiled at him. "Where else would I be?"

She was a true dark-haired, fair-skinned Irish woman. She was easily half a foot taller than Shannon, with a swan's neck, a slender frame, and sea-green eyes. You'd be forgiven for thinking she was the descendant of Irish nobility.

"I'm sorry," Michael said, "I shouldn't be here."

"Well, don't leave because of me," Elizabeth said. "You have as much right to be here as anyone."

"No, I don't," he said. "It isn't fair to you."

"Please." She put a hand on his shoulder. "Stay."

Michael had never told Shannon how things had ended with Elizabeth, but like nearly every other mystery in

Shannon's life, she had a theory—and his heroin addiction played a large part.

"Mr. Simmons," Shannon said. "Good to see you here."

"'S'up, detective." Robbie bobbed his chin at her. "You working tonight?"

"Not specifically."

Elizabeth looped her hand through the crook of Robbie's arm. "Shannon and Michael were friends of my brother's," she said. "They all practically grew up together."

"And they got you working his case?" Robbie said to Shannon. "Small world, ain't it?"

"It is, and I'd be happy to tell you more, but there's a wake we're supposed to be at right now." Shannon pulled the door to McCullough's open before Robbie asked any more questions about her ties to Colm Keane.

The four of them entered together—Elizabeth and Robbie first, then Michael, and finally, Shannon, pulling up the rear.

The rest of the wake went by uneventfully. There were drinks, food, and plenty of stories about Colm shooting his mouth off at one person, or his temper catapulting him into a fight with another.

Over the course of the evening, Shannon drank more than she had intended.

The night ended when Michael and Shannon walked back to Shannon's Jeep with Robbie in tow. He kept trying to put his hand around Shannon's waist, but even if he weren't a character witness in Colm's murder, she'd still bat him off just as hard as she did now.

She thought he was done with it until they got up to the walk in front of his house. Michael broke off from them—he walked to Shannon's Jeep to go use its electric lighter—and Robbie, perhaps knowing this was his last chance, made a move.

Before Shannon knew it, he'd spun her around so she was chest-to-chest with him. His arms squeezed her closer by the second; his breath reeked of cigarettes and cheap lager.

He smiled at her. His drunken eyes tried to keep their balance, but instead wandered all around her face.

"Stop it." She was a little tilted herself.

"Come on," he said. "Come on."

"You're with Elizabeth." She lightly pushed at him, but that didn't break his hold on her. "You two came together."

Robbie grinned at her. "She ain't here now."

The way he pawed at Shannon made it seem like he assumed her attraction to him was a foregone conclusion. He was a good-looking guy, no doubt, but all through the evening, every joke he made had fallen flat with her, every story he told was about how cool he was and how everyone loved him. He was so full of himself, it shocked her that he didn't split open.

"You know you want it." Robbie put his hand on her butt.

That was all it took. She shoved him flat. Before she knew it, she heard his head smack into the grass like a hollow melon.

Shannon got herself ready for him to come back at her—he wouldn't have been the first guy to try and get physical with her.

For a second, it looked like he was going to come after her. He sat up, tensed his mouth, balled his fists, then dry-heaved. He puked into his own lap.

"Oh my god!" She cackled at him.

Robbie flopped back into the grass, ready to pass out. She didn't want him to die—at the very least, she might need him for further questioning about Colm's murder. So Shannon turned him on his side.

"You bitch," he muttered with his eyes closed.

"You better watch your mouth. I'm within my bounds to arrest you for sexually harassing an officer." She wasn't. There was no such law she knew of.

But he didn't have to know that.

Robbie groaned. He ripped up a handful of grass and tried to toss it at her. He threw it in the wrong direction.

"Nighty night." Shannon patted him on his shaved head. One evening with Robbie Simmons would be enough to last her a lifetime.

She walked back to her Jeep, where Michael sat behind the wheel. "Did you see that?" She pointed at Robbie passed out on the lawn.

"Yep."

"All the more reason why I can't wait to get the hell out of Chicago."

Michael put the Jeep in gear and eased off the clutch.

"I'm proud you didn't have a drink," she said to him. She leaned her head back against the seat and closed her eyes. The Jeep swirled around her more than she wanted to let on.

"It's not hard to turn down something you never cared for."

Shannon opened her eyes and rolled down her window. She loved the feeling of the warm air on a summer night as she drove, and she wouldn't miss a second of it.

"Did you notice Isabella never showed up?" Michael asked.

Shannon blinked for a minute, trying to clear her head. She hadn't noticed.

"You'd think she'd be there," he said.

"Maybe they weren't what we thought."

"No," Michael said. "They were."

CHAPTER 14

Michael stopped the Jeep in front of their building. After helping his sister trip into bed, and ensuring that Frank snuggled in next to her, the real work began.

He walked back out front of their apartment and got into his own car. Shannon wouldn't mind his sneaking out at night—especially when he came back with information to jump-start her investigation.

Driving through Wrigleyville at this time of night was like diving head first into Chicago's id. It was something Michael had to prepare himself to do at times.

There were pretty girls in tight skirts, low-cut blouses, and heels almost too high to handle all the drinks they had. Young men walked in packs, cruising from bar to bar, watching the girls stumble and cackle in embarrassment. When the time was right, the two sides would meet, and work their best game on each other.

Within a minute or two, Michael drove his way out of Wrigleyville. He went south on Lake Shore Drive, traveling parallel to Lake Michigan, past the docked pleasure craft, past the twinkling lights of barges on their way to (or from) Canadian ports, past all the nice condos overlooking it all.

When he finally pulled off of Lake Shore, he didn't stray far.

There was a halfway house he knew—a place run by a fifty-something black lady who went by the name Miss Honey. He wasn't sure if her real name was Rachel or Rochelle, but it didn't matter—no one called her that.

Michael stopped his car out front. He checked himself in the mirror. He was fatter than he'd been three years ago, but still a far cry from overweight. His hair was neater, and his eyes had the life worked back in them. He set the parking break and cut the engine.

If Miss Honey didn't recognize him, that was just as well. He was better off leaving this alone. Shannon might figure out a way to solve Colm's murder, and if she didn't, they'd be in Stockholm by this time next week. Running from everything wasn't a bad option, just not one he wanted to take.

It wasn't too late to start the car again and drive away. All he had to do was turn the key. It was already in the ignition.

He fiddled with his father's cigarette case in his pocket. He eyed the brick apartment building across the street.

Colm was dead. There was no taking that back. Why should Michael risk exposing himself to the very thing that nearly ruined his life once before?

Because he had to.

He got out of the car. He locked it behind him and crossed into the worn-out courtyard of the brick apartment building he'd lived in during the darkest years of his life.

The building's glass front door was unlocked. It always was.

A guy in baggy jeans and a snow-white T-shirt sat in a ripped-up pleather chair in the lobby. He glanced at Michael as he walked in, then immediately went back to texting someone on his phone.

Michael started up the staircase.

The place hadn't changed at all since he'd been there last. The walls were still the same chocolate brown, the carpet was still that dark blue industrial stuff you'd find in the booking areas of police stations and in the back rooms of old public libraries.

When he arrived at the apartment building's top floor—the sixth floor—he looked at the door at the end of the hall.

He made his way toward it.

Nothing in a place like this stayed clean. All the doors he passed were made of faux wood paneling. Every scratch and ding, every chip missing near the doors' bottoms and sides had come from decades of hard living.

But not hers. It waited at the end of the hall, the same immaculate white it had always been.

Knowing Miss Honey, she probably had it repainted every weekend. She probably fleeced some new tenant into doing it. Come to think of it, hadn't Michael done it once?

He knocked on the door. No light shined from beneath it—not that he should expect anything else at three a.m.

He knocked again. He didn't pound or tap, just a firm knock. If she were there, she'd answer. It didn't matter what time it was.

Michael lifted his fist to knock a third time, but the door swung back a couple inches before he did.

A gun barrel looked him in the eyes.

Some kind of long revolver. It was that Colt Python Miss Honey loved so much—he was sure of it.

"That's no way to treat a former guest, is it?" he said. The door opened a bit further. A woman's sharp eyes peered at him from the darkness. They lanced him, seeing through any lie he'd try to cover himself in.

A hustler never got hustled.

It was funny, in a way. Miss Honey had a full, feminine face that almost clashed with the severity she carried in her eyes. She looked like the kind of woman who'd get you in more trouble than you bargained for if you let her.

"Michael?" The revolver lowered. "God almighty! Is that you?"

The door flew open. She beamed at him and threw her free arm around his shoulders. She squeezed him so tight, his spine popped.

"Look at you!" Miss Honey said. "I thought you was gone from here for good!"

"I thought I was, too." He smiled at her to mask his guilt. "I'm glad that didn't turn out to be true."

She returned the smile. Her eyes took on a beautiful sparkle after seeing Michael—something that gave hint to the keen mind behind them. To be one of her marks might have almost been worth the heartache and the financial ruin.

"May I come in?" he asked.

"Of course!" She waved him in with the Python. The pistol was almost as big as her arm. "No sense in you standing out in the damn hallway all night, is there?"

"No, I don't think so."

The inside of Miss Honey's apartment was just as he remembered it. On the far wall, beneath a picture window, she had her old RCA Hi-Fi. It looked the same as the day it was fresh off the line in 1973. Her records had been neatly categorized into coffee-colored shelves that stretched from floor to ceiling. There must've been a couple hundred at least.

She had the same burnt orange paint on the walls, and the same light green shag carpet. A mural painted by someone who'd come through the halfway house in the eighties still hung off the wall.

"I'm going to get some tea going," she said. "You care for a cup?" She had her cell phone in-hand. She texted someone.

"I'd love one," Michael said. "What have you got?"

"Green, chrysanthemum, jasmine, black, and some junk somebody got me from the mall a couple years back that smells like rat poison."

"I'll just have the green," he said.

She smiled and nodded, then held up her phone. "Was the fella down in the lobby awake when you came in?"

"Yeah." Michael took a seat on the corduroy couch to his left.

"Good," she said. "I was worried he wasn't gonna keep an eye on the door like I told him to. Hard to find somebody worth their salt these days."

She disappeared behind the partition wall that separated her kitchen from the rest of her apartment.

Michael peeked at her bookshelf. It was packed with all kinds of big, intellectual books—books that made great roach-smashers in a pinch. Stuff by philosophers like Sarte and Nieztche, and big classics like *Gone with the Wind*. She had smaller books too—he noticed *Fahrenheit*

451 and *The Grapes of Wrath*. All the mandatory high school stuff that had almost turned him away from novels years ago.

Every book was dog-eared to hell, or had little colored strips of paper popping out of their tops. Who knew what use a woman like Miss Honey had for them.

"I didn't know you liked Aldous Huxley," Michael said. "I thought you were more into authors who were a hundred years dead."

"I like Hemingway," she said. "He died in the sixties."

"You know, I almost dropped out of high school when they made us read *Brave New World*." He pulled the book off the shelf and flipped through the pages.

"It's not Huxley's best book," Miss Honey said. "I guess I read it because I agreed with the man's philosophy more than his work."

"And what philosophy was that?" Michael flipped the book over and glanced at the back cover.

"He was all about treating your fellow human being with proper decency," she said. "That's something I can get behind."

"You always were a bleeding heart," Michael said. "I never understood why."

She popped her head around the corner and looked at him with disbelief. "You benefited from this bleeding heart pretty well."

He smiled at her. "You know, on my way up here, I wondered if I'd be able to get a rise out of you as easily as I did three years ago."

She mock-scowled at him, then disappeared into the kitchen again.

"Read anything published in the last ten years?" Michael asked.

"Nothing worth talking about," she said. "Just a whole lot of things from people more in love with their words than what they have to say."

"That's harsh."

"You know I don't pull no punches."

No, she never did. Except when you had more money than sense—then she'd tell you anything you wanted to hear.

"You been keeping up with your reading like I told you to?" she asked.

"I try to." He put the book back on the shelf.

"Don't lie to me. You know damn well that anyone who wants to read does it. Anybody who says they try ain't really trying at all."

"I missed you lecturing me," he said. "I'm sorry I showed up like this out of nowhere. I know it wasn't right to come here in the middle of the night."

"No apologizing," Miss Honey said. "When you left, I told you that you was always welcome to stop by any time you wanted. I meant that."

"I know you did. But I should've called or said hello a long time ago."

She stepped out from her kitchen, two bone-white teacups in hand. She smiled at Michael as she handed one to him. "You did what you had to do." She grabbed a bottle of honey and squeezed some into her tea. "And I know you couldn't have done it here. I'm just glad to see you clean and happy, however that came to you."

"It took my sister knocking sense into me."

"Ain't that how it always is?"

Michael took a sip of his tea. "Play any good pool halls lately?" he said into his cup.

She lifted her eyes to him and shrugged. "Some old fellas play in a hall closer to the lake, but they ain't got a thing on my game. Nice thing about playing them is, any of them get a hot streak and I just throw a little wink their way or drop my neckline a little bit, and that takes care of that."

"What about the younger ones?" he asked.

She narrowed her eyes at him. "You think I ain't got what they want?"

He smiled at her.

"A lot of them got more money than sense," she said. "'Course, most of the same rules apply to them as the old fellas. Probably the only thing a twenty-year-old and a fifty-year-old got in common is their big head shuts off when their little starts getting ideas."

Michael couldn't argue. He held his teacup up, and she clinked hers against his. They both took their sips.

When he lowered his cup, he noticed her staring at him. "What?" he asked.

She smirked at him. "I know you didn't come here at three in the morning to drink tea and talk about me hustling pool halls. So why don't you just come out with it already?"

"You're right," he said. "I came for book chat."

She laughed. "Boy, I know the only people knocking on that door at this time are fellas looking for booty, or people looking to hear what I have to say."

"Aren't I listening to you?"

"You know what I mean."

He sat his teacup on her coffee table. "I still can't get one by you, can I?"

"Nobody can," she said. "That's why I'm still here in my ratchety palace."

"You like this place."

"That ain't got nothing to do with why you're here."

"No," he said, "it doesn't."

"Then are you gonna ask me what you came to ask me, or do I have to go get my gun from the counter?"

He drummed his fingers on the steel cigarette case in his pocket. Time to put up or shut up. "Shannon wouldn't like it if she knew I were here right now."

"I wouldn't like it either, if I were her," Miss Honey said. "You were a damn mess when she took you out of here. You couldn't go a day without sticking a needle in your arm—even if I did get you to stop doing that in my building."

He chuckled. "You know how scared I was the first time you caught me shooting up downstairs?" Michael nodded toward her revolver. "I thought you were going to blow my head off."

"So did I," Miss Honey said. "But I knew by the way you talked, and by the look in your eye, that there was still something in you—that I'd be losing it if I treated you like another broke-down junkie." She prodded his breastbone with her French-tipped fingernail. "You can't hide nothing from me."

Michael wished she was right—that he still had something in him which made him more than another addict. Maybe she *was* right. He could've killed himself a hundred times over with his heroin, and he'd certainly wanted to at times. But he never had.

"So, what'd you come to ask me?" she said.

"You know anything about a white guy getting shot near 46th and Ashland on Thursday? Over by a liquor store?"

Miss Honey pulled in her lips and leaned back on the couch. She tapped her nails against the porcelain teacup while she thought. "No," she said. "No, I ain't really heard a thing about that." She sighed. "The way the city's been the last few years … there's too much happening for me to keep a hold on hardly any of it."

He should've expected that. How many murders had happened already this year? Three hundred and fifty? One woman running a halfway house near Lake Michigan couldn't possibly keep her fingers in all of it.

"Know anything about a Mexican girl?" Michael asked. "Goes by the name of Isabella Arroz?"

Miss Honey's lips moved to one side of her face as she put her arm on the back of the couch. "Now that might be something we can work with," she said. "That name—Arroz—sounds familiar. What else you know about this girl?"

Michael shrugged. "Practically nothing."

"Now, I never known that to be true." She smiled at him. "Plenty of times folk say they don't know nothing about something, but things start to pop in their head anyhow. I'm sure you know how that is."

He returned the smile. "I think she's got a brother—or a cousin she's close with," Michael said. He remembered seeing another man in nearly every picture Colm had with Isabella on his Facebook page. He looked close to her, but not like he was her husband or man-in-waiting.

"He got a face?"

"Yeah," Michael said. "He's short, got a shaved head. Looks like a dude who'd stab you if you looked at him when he was in a bad mood. He's missing part of his left ear."

Miss Honey snapped her fingers. "Afonso," she said.

"You know him?"

"What's Isabella look like?"

"Tall, thin. She's got straight, dark hair, and I bet she'd give you a run for your money when it comes to getting men to do what she wants."

"A Mexican Helen of Troy," Miss Honey said. "I seen her."

Michael could hardly believe it. Surely, she had to be thinking of someone else. "How do you know it was her?"

"I wouldn't forget somebody like her," she said. "She should be laying out on some rich fella's cabin cruiser in New Buffalo. Instead, I seen her hanging out at the clubs with Afonso. Only caught her first name at the time."

"So?" Michael asked. "How you are so sure the girl you saw wasn't some other Isabella?"

"When you been around those places as long as I have," Miss Honey said, "you see crowds come and go. You get to know people's faces and names and habits. Afonso puts the moves on any girl inside a drink's throw of him—and he ain't always nice about it neither."

Miss Honey grinned. Something told Michael she had a little first-hand experience with Afonso's moves.

"He ain't ever done that to this girl Isabella, though. He's always holding the door for her, chasing other fellas away, and talking real gentle to her," Miss Honey said. "That's how I know they're each other's people."

Michael considered Miss Honey's story. How many thousands of faces made their way through her halfway house at some point? He'd bet his life that she remembered them all.

The chances that she was mistaken about Isabella Arroz and this guy Afonso being related were almost non-existent.

Still….

"You're sure?" he asked.

"Boy, you can't be knowing people like I do and forget a face," she said. "That's bad business."

Not a hint of doubt in her voice.

"Okay. So what do you know about Afonso?"

"He ain't a dude most people want to trifle with," she said. "But on the other hand, you ain't, either."

"Those are all just rumors."

"I'm betting more than a couple are true." She held her gaze on him for a moment.

He looked over at her record collection.

"Afonso is a hustler," she said. "He runs a set for the Kings. Folks say he and his boys hang out in some house near 44th and Wood. I ain't been over there."

Michael nodded. "How many guys with him?"

"I dunno," she shrugged. "Probably four or five he actually deals with, maybe a dozen or two who just come and go—you know how it is. All I got for sure is his people are in drugs. They got a couple arsons behind them—a few bodies, too—but mostly drugs."

Aside from the arsons, Afonso and his clique sounded pretty average to Michael. Nothing to be scared of.

"You hear anything about him working with a white kid named Colm?"

"Nothing pops up in my head."

He didn't think she would know, but he had to ask.

Then, Miss Honey's face darkened. "Hold on." Her eyebrows pushed together. "You ain't talking about Ewan Keane's boy, are you?"

Michael nodded. "He was the kid shot near 46th and Ashland."

Miss Honey flopped back into the couch like she'd almost fainted. She sat up. "You're telling me that the son of an Irish mobster got popped on the South Side?"

"That's what my sister tells me," Michael said.

"Why ain't you say that when you knocked on the door?" She moved her hands and her head—she was animated when she was mad. "They're gonna come down here looking for answers from somebody—and people around here ain't really want to talk to *none* of them."

"You're talking to me," Michael said.

"Don't make a joke." She slapped his knee. "They're gonna drop bodies while they look for answers. And they ain't gonna stay up that way when they do it. They're gonna tear up every neighborhood from Humboldt to Hammond, and I care about those places. Good people live there. I know you and everyone else in this city don't believe that, but I do."

"That's what I'm trying to avoid," Michael said. "I have it on good authority the Irish Mob is going to let CPD handle Colm's murder, but you and I both know their patience will only last so long."

"Boy, don't come in here and try to pass me lies!"

"I don't want to see anyone innocent get hurt," he said. "You might not believe it, but you rubbed off on me more than you realize."

She looked at him with mistrust in her eyes. "Boy, I know you're working with Keane again," she said. "That's your 'good authority,' ain't it?"

The words came at him like a slap across his cheek. He almost didn't know how to handle it. But if Miss Honey was half as good at detecting lies as she claimed to be, she'd believe him if he told the truth.

"I'm not working for him," he said. "Not anymore."

"Then why are you so worried about his boy?"

"Look," Michael said, "I'm not going back to working with him or any of his associates ever again. You think I did heroin because I liked myself back then?"

"You tell me."

"I've learned a lot about what it means to be an addict. I know there's an inner addict in me, and that son of a bitch wants me to melt my brains out of my ears. I know the only way he gets control of me is if I go back to working for Keane and all the other bosses. I'm never doing that again."

Miss Honey tilted her head back. She dissected him with her eyes. He could feel her pulling apart his shell, all the things he hid himself beneath, on her way to getting at what lay underneath.

"Then why'd you come here right now?" she asked. "From where I'm sitting, it looks like you're about two steps away from your old life."

"No," Michael said, "I'm not. It's different this time."

"It ain't no different." Miss Honey shook her head and laughed. "You're always who you are."

Maybe she had a point. Why was this any different? Was he doing this just to grab another cheap thrill he'd denied himself the past few years?

"I said you can't get nothing past me."

"It's the truth. I'm not doing this for myself anymore," he said. "I'm doing this to help Shannon."

CHAPTER 15

Father John Misty's album, *I Love You, Honeybear*, helped Shannon work through her hangover the morning after Colm's wake. She sat at her desk in the Violent Crimes Unit bullpen at the CPD office over on Blue Island Avenue.

She tried her best to focus on her computer screen. She had a slew of reports and notes to file about the murder scene itself—not to mention their search of Colm's house.

Her email client chirped at her. Shannon tabbed over and saw a new message. Her request for forensic analysis of the shell casings and cigarette butts from the scene of Colm's murder had been received by CPD's forensics lab, but the tests hadn't been run yet.

That wasn't surprising. She'd be lucky to get the results before tomorrow.

She tabbed back to the departmental database software and entered Colm's DOB for the umpteeth time. The way Chicago had been in the last decade, one would think the higher-ups would figure out a way to cut down all the paperwork for CPD's detectives. But here she was, eyeballs burning already from staring at her computer screen for the last three hours.

Someone tapped her on the shoulder.

Shannon swiveled around in her chair and saw Dedrick smiling at her. She felt a tickle in her stomach as she took her earbuds out.

"You look particularly fresh this morning," he said. "Did the wake go well last night?"

"I can still taste the rum and Coke in the back of my throat."

He sipped his coffee and laughed. "It's no hair-of-the-dog, but I bet I can scrounge up a couple beers from our colleagues' desks if that helps," he said.

"I'd puke on your shoes if I were a lesser person."

"That's no way to treat someone trying to do you a favor." Dedrick leaned up against her desk and crossed his legs at the ankles. His shoes were perfectly shined and the little light blue diamonds on his black socks exactly matched the color of his dress shirt. "You find anything new about Colm's girlfriend?"

"Isabella?"

He nodded.

"Only that she wasn't there last night."

"You didn't ask around about her?"

"Once or twice, but no one really knew her," she said. "I got the impression that more people were there to be seen by Ewan Keane rather than honor the memory of his son."

Dedrick produced a pocket-sized notebook.

"Well, I ran her name," he licked his thumb, then flipped through the pages, "and unless she's a sixty-two-year-old woman who can't seem to keep the neighborhood dogs out of her garden, or possibly a missing girl from 2008, we don't have anything on her."

Shannon closed her eyes. The room started to spin again. "So we've got virtually no chance of finding her."

"Not all is lost," Dedrick said. "We can still speak with Ewan, right?"

"He welcomes it," she said. "So much that I'm certain we aren't going to find out anything from him." She swiveled in her chair and opened the top drawer of her desk. She took out Ewan's card, then handed it to Dedrick.

"The business card of a mobster." He turned it around in his fingers. "I bet there's some collector on the internet who'd give you at least a twenty for this."

She snatched it back from him. "I'll keep that in mind."

"So, what's the point in talking to Ewan if you think he isn't going to help?"

She shrugged. "We might get lucky and see something he doesn't want us to see. Or maybe we can trip him up."

"Or maybe we can get a Bloody Mary into you."

A little puke welled up in her throat. She swallowed it back. "You put alcohol near me today," Shannon said, "you'll need a whole new outfit."

He smiled at her. Dedrick opened his mouth to say something else, but before he could, her desk phone rang.

She picked it up. "Detective Rourke."

"Shannon, this is Sergeant Daly down at the front desk. I've got a pregnant lady here asking for the detective working Colm Keane's murder case."

Her heart skipped a beat. No way she'd get this lucky. "What's her name?"

There was a little noise on the other side of the line while Sergeant Daly asked the woman her name.

"Isabella Arroz," he said.

CHAPTER 16

When the elevator doors opened to the first floor, Shannon ran as fast as her hangover would allow. Dedrick followed behind her, the leather soles of his shoes pounding against the tiled floor with every hurried step.

She rounded a corner and nearly crashed into an officer who side-stepped her. She saw Isabella up ahead, beyond a set of glass security doors.

Shannon slowed down. It was best to not appear too eager when a witness like Isabella surfaced. People picked up on nerves, and became nervous themselves, forgetting key facts or keeping information from an investigator. It didn't take a genius to figure out how badly that could damage an investigation.

She checked that her periwinkle blouse was neatly tucked in the waistband of her gray slacks. Satisfied, Shannon pushed open the security door.

Isabella's coffee-colored eyes fell on her immediately. In person, she was so beautiful it was almost unsettling—even for Shannon. It was certainly unfair. She was a walking statue, the kind of thing an artist would've chiseled out of marble over a decade of work.

She looked back at Dedrick. He already had a little perspiration on his brow. He looked scared as the computer club president asking a girl to prom.

"Isabella?" Shannon stuck out her hand. "I'm Detective Shannon Rourke."

"Hello." Isabella took her hand.

"This is Detective Dedrick Halman; he's been assisting me with Colm's case."

Dedrick smiled tensely and waved at her. He was crushing on her. It took all the control Shannon was able to muster to keep herself from rolling her eyes at him.

"If it's all right with you, we'd like you to come upstairs with us and talk for a few minutes."

"That's fine," Isabella said.

"Then follow us this way, please."

The security door unlocked and automatically swung open, courtesy of Sergeant Daly. The three of them walked through, the detectives flanking Isabella.

Shannon waited until the door snapped shut behind them to speak. "I have to say, Isabella, you're somewhat of an enigma over here."

"Am I in trouble?" She sounded scared. Not uncommon for someone with no record walking into this set of circumstances.

"No," Shannon said. "I only wanted to talk to you about Colm. I thought you'd be at his wake last night— but now I know why." Shannon nodded toward Isabella's belly. "How far along are you?"

"Six months," Isabella said. "And I feel like my spine is going to break in half."

"You carry it well." When she wasn't pregnant, Shannon guessed Isabella was somewhere around a size two.

They rounded the corner and walked past the administrative offices on their way back to the elevator.

Suddenly, Isabella stopped.

"Is something wrong?" Shannon turned toward her. God help them if her water just broke or something.

Isabella didn't appear to be in pain. She looked like she'd seen a ghost. Her eyes were fixed on the end of the hall.

"Do you need us to get someone?" Shannon asked.

"No," she said. "I'm fine."

Shannon and Dedrick glanced at each other.

"Would you still like to go upstairs with us?" Shannon asked.

"Who's up there?"

"A whole flock of detectives."

That seemed to bother her worse than anything.

"Will they hear us when we talk?"

"What are you planning on saying?" Shannon asked.

Isabella knotted her fingers together. When she did, she made her arms into a sling beneath her belly. She couldn't keep her eyes off the floor.

"Something," she bit her lip, "I don't want people to hear. You know? People who might know Colm's Dad?"

"I understand." Shannon wasn't about to tell her that *she* knew Ewan. "If it makes you feel better, we can go somewhere private and talk."

Isabella pulled her lips in, thinking, then nodded.

They walked to the elevator in silence. It carried them to the third floor, back to the Violent Crimes division offices. There were a couple private interrogation rooms along the far wall.

Dedrick opened up the nearest one.

"Suite number one," he said. He held his arm across his body like a bellhop at a five-star hotel.

Shannon followed Isabella in. She rolled her eyes at Dedrick. She'd had to save that one for far too long.

He mouthed the word, "What?" at her.

"We'll talk about it later."

The door clicked shut behind them. The bone-white walls of the interrogation room were bare. The room itself would've been empty, save for an old chair and table at its center. The table was bolted into the ground and had locking hooks which the detectives could feed the links of handcuffs into for their rowdier interviews.

That wouldn't be necessary today. Isabella looked like she'd wilt if Shannon breathed on her too hard.

"Have a seat, if you like." Shannon held a hand toward the plastic chair pushed in at the faux-wood table.

Dedrick pulled it out for her.

"Thank you." Isabella settled into it.

"Don't mention it." He smiled at her.

As she watched that little display, Shannon's hangover inexplicably felt ten times worse. She steadied herself against a wall and crossed her arms, bracing herself for another random burst of chivalry from Dedrick.

"Is it Colm's?" Shannon asked.

Isabella looked at her in shock. "Of course."

"How long had you and Colm been together?"

"Eight months—if that matters to your investigation."

"We're not here to pass judgment on you," Dedrick said too quickly. "If Detective Rourke or I ask you a question, you can be sure it's because it has something to do with catching Colm's murderer."

Dedrick was a far cry from the ready-to-rumble bad cop he'd been with Robbie Simmons.

"I understand." Isabella rested her arms on top of her pregnant stomach. "But I don't like feeling judged."

"I'm sure that wasn't Detective Rourke's intent," Dedrick said.

Shannon nodded. "Barring anything too personal," she said, "would you mind telling us what it was you were afraid to say downstairs?"

Isabella knotted her fingers again. She played with a ring on her pinkie, twisting it, then pulling and pushing it over her knuckle.

"Anything you say here stays between you, me, and Detective Halman," Shannon said. "You don't have to worry about anyone else hearing it until we go to trial."

"I know." Isabella took a deep breath and nodded.

"So, would you like to tell us what you know?"

She nodded again. A strand of her straight, black hair dropped over her eyes. She sat up in her chair and pushed it behind her ear.

"Ewan had Colm killed," she said.

CHAPTER 17

Michael did his best junkie walk.

It wasn't too hard to remember how. You just had to act like your joints were made out of broken glass, like you hadn't had an honest meal in three days, and like your underwear was bound up with cold sweat—or hot, depending on your drug of choice.

For him, it had been heroin. He'd loved to feel the pain-melting joy when the drug slithered through his veins, coiled around his gray matter, and sifted through his ganglia.

He wasn't on it now, of course. He never would be again, for all the damage it did to his relationship to everything outside of himself. Not just his relationship with his sister, per se, or his failed engagement to Elizabeth, or running from the only man who had ever really treated him like a son—but his relationship with everything that was *not* Michael Rourke. His connection to reality. His perceptions of what true happiness was.

Funny. Most people assumed all the damage came from the drug itself, or from what you'd do to scrape together money for another fix, or even the damage of yanking away a chemical that your body had grown dependent on to survive. Withdrawals were bad, stealing an old lady's toaster for a few bucks was terrible, and having the body of a sixty-year-old at age thirty-five wasn't fun.

But the hardest thing to suffer was Michael's ability to ever discern *true* joy from a quick fix tied to a fishhook.

That was the drug's damage.

For the first time in nearly three years, he carried that damage in his walk again. Although, this time, it was intentional.

And his walk carried him across 44th street. He'd parked his car over on the far side of Davis Square Park, so Afonso and whoever he worked with wouldn't think he was just another bored white boy from the north side—which was a category he probably fit in, if he were honest with himself.

An old house with sun-bleached blue siding watched over the corner of 44th and Wood. On its big, concrete front porch, a pair of guys in their early twenties sat in folding chairs—one skinny, one fat. They played cards and drank.

Nice and relaxed. Good.

A kid leaned up against the side of the house with his hands in his pockets. He was probably ten or twelve. He'd know exactly where the street stash was. He'd hid it, after all. A few feet away, a teenager in saggy jeans and a long, black T-shirt sat on the front steps of the house. He nodded at Michael. The kid knew that anyone who moved and looked like Michael did right now would be here for one thing.

Michael shambled over the curb and up into the short stretch of dried-out lawn in front of the house.

"Need a taste?" the teenager asked.

"Horse." Michael nodded. "I got twenty."

"A'ight, man. Chill here."

The teenager looked around the corner of the house. He nodded to the little kid and touched his hand to his shoulder. The little kid scurried off around back of the house. Michael already knew where. He had their stash tucked under the wheel well of a '72 Buick LeSabre on concrete blocks in the back—somebody's passion project.

"Got your money?" the teenager asked.

"Yeah." Michael whipped his arm around the back of his waist. The teenager reacted faster than he expected. Maybe it was his youth, or maybe it was just that the kid had grown so accustomed to the way a person's arm bent around themselves when they grabbed a gun. Whatever the cause, he was halfway across the yard before anyone else realized Michael had just pulled out a handgun—his Taurus Judge.

The two guys up on the porch stood. The fat man reached behind his back—the same motion Michael had just made.

Michael squeezed the trigger on his Judge.

It didn't take careful aim to hit Fat. Not at this range. Triple-aught buckshot pellets ripped out of the barrel. At least one hit him.

Fat dropped to the ground, screaming and clutching his knee.

Michael pointed his Judge at Skinny.

"Pull the trigger," Michael said, calm as a deacon at Sunday dinner.

Skinny was a little slower on the draw. His thumb rested on the safety of his pistol. His eyes were wide as dinner plates and glued to his screaming friend. Did he even notice Michael?

He pointed the Judge at the soffit above Skinny's head, then fired. Half-rotted splinters of compression board and tufts of insulation rained down over him.

"Unless you want to end up like him, throw me the money."

Skinny stared at Michael, dumbfounded.

"Toss the gun in the yard, and get the money," Michael said.

Skinny nodded. His mouth hung open and his lower lip jiggled when he did. He tossed his gun over the side of the porch, then he stooped down and rifled through Fat's pockets.

"What the hell you doing, man? Afonso gonna kick our asses!" Fat yelled.

Skinny shrugged and tossed a roll of bills to Michael.

"He's saving your ass is what he's doing." Michael held the money up. He looked at Skinny. "Let Afonso know that if he wants this back, he needs to come meet me alone over in the park."

"We ain't telling nobody nothing," Fat said. "Don't do what he says!"

"I got to, man." Skinny gave him a helpless look. "You know Afonso wants his money."

"I don't care, man!" Fat howled. "Dude shot me in the knee, and you gonna help him? Grab your tool and smoke him!"

Skinny stared at Michael. His eyes swiped over to where he'd tossed the gun in the yard, but a split second later, they were on Michael again.

"I've got enough in this thing to get your knees, too," Michael said to Skinny. "And his other knee, and at least your manhood, if you think about picking up that handgun again. Actually, I'm not too sure about that last one. The shot tends to spread with this little Judge. I might accidentally put a couple pellets in your gut."

"He's lying, man," Fat said. "He ain't got the heart to shoot you."

Michael laughed. Fat laid on his back with a knee turned into ground pork, and he thought Michael didn't have the guts to shoot the skinny kid?

"You know, you don't get to a hospital soon, you're gonna lose that whole leg," Michael said. "I've seen it happen. It's not pretty."

"Shut up or I'm gonna blow your head off, you junkie bitch!" Fat said. He had quite a vocabulary.

"No, you're not," Michael said. "You're going to the hospital, and while your friend here drives you, he's going to call Afonso and let him know I'd like to talk to him."

"He ain't gonna talk to you," Fat said. "He's gonna work your ass."

"Not if he wants his money back."

"You think he's gonna sit down with you because you got a little of his money?" Fat laughed. "That's two grand, man—that ain't nothing."

Michael grimaced. "You're right." He looked at Skinny, who flinched as soon as Michael laid eyes on him. "You got a stash? Maybe right inside the front door there?"

"Don't you do nothing he says!" Fat yelled.

Michael marched up the steps and tapped Fat's wounded knee with the bottom of his shoe. Fat howled like a street cat.

"Give me the stash," Michael said. "If Afonso asks you what happened, say this one—" he pointed at Fat "—gave it up for a deep dish."

Skinny nodded. He opened the front door just wide enough to reach in and pull out a black trash bag.

It clinked with glass when he handed it over to Michael.

He peeked into the bag. The veins in his arms pounded. They ached for what was inside—little baggies of heroin intermixed with glass vials holding crack and meth.

Michael closed his eyes tight. He'd have to put this temptation away if he wanted to find out who killed Colm. It was only a moment before the desire to shoot every baggie of heroin into the pits of his elbows, the veins around his wrists, and even the little places between his toes, passed.

He closed the bag.

"There's, what, twenty grand worth of product in here?" Michael jingled the bag.

"Something like that," Skinny said.

"You think your boy Afonso will come talk to me if I hide this from him?"

"Yeah," Skinny said.

"Okay then, let him know I'd like to talk to him about Colm Keane." Michael backed down the steps, keeping the Judge pointed at Skinny. "It's very important you remember that name. Say it."

"Colm Keane," Skinny said.

Fat moaned in pain.

"Good." Michael said. "Now turn around and keep saying it."

"Colm Keane," Skinny said. He turned his nose to the house. "Colm Keane. Colm Keane."

"You're doing great!" Michael said from the far side of a car parked out front of the house. "Don't forget: I'll be at the park."

"Colm Keane," Skinny responded.

CHAPTER 18

Silence pushed in from the interrogation room's white walls. Shannon and Dedrick looked at each other, wide-eyed. The idea that they might have a witness here who could help them pin a credible murder against a captain of the Irish Mob was a lot to process—ignoring the moral implications of a man killing his own son.

"Detective?" Isabella glanced at Shannon.

"Saying that Ewan had Colm killed is a big accusation to make." Shannon stood up from where she'd been leaning against the wall. "Do you know why he would've done that?"

"You don't believe me?" Already a tear welled up on the edge of Isabella's eyelid.

Dedrick appeared at her side in a heartbeat. "No," he said. "What Detective Rourke means is we're just a little surprised, is all. It took a lot of courage to come forward like you have."

Isabella nodded. She sniffled and dabbed at her eyes with her fingertips. She was trying to keep the tears from ruining her makeup, but mascara had already started to run from her eyelids.

Dedrick reached into his pocket and gave her a handkerchief. Of course he had one. The guy pictured himself the modern incarnation of Sidney Poitier.

Isabella took it and wiped under her eyes. Black splotches of mascara stained it. "Great." She sputtered a laugh between her tears. She held the handkerchief up for him to take. "I'm sorry I ruined it."

"It's all right." Dedrick smiled at her. "You hang onto that for a minute."

She swallowed and balled the handkerchief in her fist. "Colm stole from his father," Isabella said.

"How do you know that?" Shannon said.

"It's my fault." Isabella's hands pulled the handkerchief like she wanted to rip it apart. "I pushed him into it."

Shannon looked at Dedrick, but he had his eyes fixed on Isabella. It was like he hadn't heard what she said—or maybe he didn't find it a little dubious.

"So you came here to confess your involvement in a robbery?" Shannon asked.

Isabella balled up her fists and cried harder this time. She was scared. And she had every reason to be. No matter which side she played—CPD or the Irish Mob—she was in danger.

"I don't think it would be wise to prosecute Isabella for a robbery," Dedrick said. "Given that she's willingly come forward with information about a murder."

Why would he say that outright? The threat of an arrest for her involvement in the robbery could have been the leverage they needed to get good information out of Isabella. Did he have to say that in front of her? He couldn't step outside and talk to Shannon about something like that?

Of course they weren't going to arrest her.

"I'd rather leave that decision up to the State's Attorney's office," Shannon said, "*after* we've finished hearing what Isabella has to say."

She turned her attention back to Isabella.

"So, you say Colm stole something from his father. What was it?"

Isabella took a breath to relax herself. Then she was back to her fingers again. She stared at them. She weaved the handkerchief between her knuckles and picked at her fingernails. "Money," she said at a whisper.

"How much?"

"Colm said it was eighty thousand." She looked down at the handkerchief again.

"Where is it now?"

"I don't know. No matter how many times I asked him, he wouldn't tell me." She wiped her nose. "We thought it'd be enough to start a new life in Canada together." She met Shannon's eyes and tried to smile through her tears. She barked a sharp laugh at herself. "We were stupid," she said. "You don't rob a man like Ewan and get away with it—no matter who you are to him."

No question. And Colm should've known that.

Shannon remembered what her brother had said about Colm's demeanor the last few months—that he was on edge, that everything seemed wrong, until, suddenly, it all wasn't. He'd turned some kind of corner which had made him relax—probably that was when he'd stolen the money. Furthermore, stealing money from his father matched with what Robbie had told them.

"Why did the two of you need to go to Canada?" Shannon asked. "Why not stay here?"

"Colm couldn't get away from his problems if we stayed here," she said. "We both knew that."

"His drinking?" Dedrick asked.

She nodded.

"You think he would've quit if he left for Canada?"

"He promised he would," Isabella said. "He'd been going to meetings since we found out I was pregnant, but I know he slipped up a couple times."

Shannon and Dedrick gave each other a dubious look.

"And you believed that leaving the country was the only way to keep Colm sober?" Shannon said.

"His sponsor thought it would. Colm said the guy was leaving Chicago. He was going to live in Stockholm, where he'd get a chance to start over without all the baggage from his addictions. We both thought if it worked for him, it'd work for Colm, too."

Shannon's stomach sank to her knees. The hangover couldn't hold a candle to what she felt now. If Michael realized he'd planted the idea of starting over in a new country into Colm's head, he wouldn't be able to live with the guilt. Shannon feared he might turn to heroin again.

"That's funny," Dedrick said. "Detective Rourke and her brother are set to leave for Stockholm in a couple days."

"Michael was Colm's sponsor," Shannon said.

That hung in the air for a moment. Shannon expected Isabella to cry harder, or shoot her a dirty look. But to her surprise, Isabella didn't react at all.

"When were you supposed to leave for Canada?" Shannon asked.

"Yesterday morning."

"Did Colm pack a bag?" she asked. "Clothes? Toiletries? That sort of thing?"

"I have it in the back of my brother's car," Isabella said. "It's out in the parking lot if you want to see it."

"Take us to it."

Isabella dabbed at her face with the handkerchief one last time before she worked her way up from her chair—the baby must've weighed more than it looked. She followed Dedrick and Shannon out of the room.

Outside the station, the sun beat down. The day was clear and humid, and thank God they didn't have to leave the shade of the concrete parking garage. Shannon beat back another wave of nausea.

"The car's over there." Isabella pointed at a black Chrysler 300.

The car was like an oil stain against the gray concrete walls. It had black paint, black rims, and windows tinted black as chalkboards. The car was in pristine condition, save a crack in the rear windshield that stretched from one side to the other.

As they got closer, Shannon noticed the engine was running.

"Is someone in the car?"

"My brother," Isabella answered. "Afonso."

The driver side window lowered. A man talking on his cell phone scowled out at Isabella, waiting for her to say something.

Shannon recognized Afonso from a couple of the Facebook pictures she'd seen. He'd looked hard then, and he looked worse in person. The guy had a face you could start a match off of. Part of his left ear was missing, and the skin beneath it was scarred, as if his ear had been cut off or something similarly gruesome.

"Pop the trunk," Isabella said.

The trunk popped up. She lifted it open. Inside were some children's toys, an emergency road kit, some other odds and ends like window cleaner and a couple hand towels, and an olive-green army surplus duffel bag.

"Is that Colm's?" Dedrick asked.

Isabella pulled it out with one hand.

"Seems awful light for someone getting ready to move their entire life to a new country," he said.

"Colm didn't want to take too many things with him. He said if we crossed the border with everything we had, it'd look suspicious. He was afraid they'd search us and maybe find our money. He promised we'd buy whatever we needed when we got there."

"Then he had Ewan's money with him," Shannon said.

"I don't think so," Isabella said. "We got into a fight that night. About the money."

"What happened?"

"He didn't bring it with him," she said, "and like I told you before, he wouldn't tell me where it was. He didn't trust me. I felt like, I'm starting my life over with this person, and he wasn't being honest with me. I have a problem with liars."

"Did you two make up?"

Isabella tucked a strand of hair behind her ear. Then she knotted her fingers together again. "No, not before he…." She closed her eyes and a tear squeezed out.

"Before he went to the liquor store?"

She nodded.

A child's crying came from the back of the car.

"Ugh." Isabella shook her head. She was at the car's rear passenger-side door in a flash. She threw it open.

Shannon peeked into the door, over Isabella's shoulder. There were two children strapped into the back of the car, one crying and one smiling. Sopping tears rolled down the little girl's face. Her feet kicked over the edge of her booster seat.

"Marti took Reina!" she said.

A doll laid at the little boy's feet.

"I told you two to be quiet." Isabella reached across the girl and grabbed the doll from the floor of the car. She threw it back on the girl's lap, and jammed a finger in the boy's face. "I told you to cut it out," she said to him. "And if I hear another word out of either of you, you're both picking out switches when we get home. Got it?"

"Yes, ma'am." Both children nodded their heads.

Isabella closed the door, then rejoined Shannon and Dedrick at the back of the car. "You try to be nice and they just take advantage."

"That's all right," Dedrick said. "I don't think my kids would last ten minutes sitting out in the garage here."

"Oh, they aren't my children," she said.

"You a nanny?" Dedrick sounded a little surprised.

"No, they're my little sister and brother. They're usually good kids."

"Where are your parents?" Shannon said.

"My father left us six years ago, and my mother has been gone for four years. I've been a mother to these two since I was nineteen."

"I know exactly what that's like," Shannon said. "My father was a mean drunk and my mother may as well have never been around."

Isabella rested her hand on Shannon's arm. She gave her a little look of commiseration.

"Hey, Bella!" Afonso was off his phone. He had the front passenger window rolled down. "We gotta go!"

She shot him a dirty look. "I still have more to say to the detectives."

"It's an emergency," he said. "Auntie Maria is sick."

"What?" Isabella looked at him like he'd just spouted total nonsense.

"Now, girl," he said. "We gotta go before she's really hurt."

"If you need to leave," Shannon said, "we can continue this when it's best for you. Would you mind giving us your name and address?"

"Got some paper?"

Dedrick pulled out his pocket notebook and a pen. He handed them both to her. She wrote her information down and handed it back to him.

"You want to talk to me or Detective Rourke, you call this number right here." He passed her a business card.

"I will." Isabella opened the front passenger door. "Thank you, detectives."

As soon as she closed the door behind her, Afonso's car took off. He drove down to the front gate of the garage like he was being chased. He laid on his horn until the attendant raised the boom and let the car out. He floored it down the street.

"Well, she was nice," Dedrick said.

Shannon rolled her eyes.

CHAPTER 19

After ending their conversation with Isabella, Shannon and Dedrick wasted no time getting to Ewan Keane's office.

The Galway Tap, the restaurant where he kept his office, was a short drive northeast from the CPD station on Blue Island. When they arrived at Keane's restaurant in Boystown, Dedrick pulled up to the curb along the front of the building and parked—a rarity. Shannon couldn't remember ever finding a parking spot that easily in this part of town.

"What are the odds Ewan Keane tells us anything we want to know?" Dedrick said as he turned off the car.

"He'll have to tell us something." Shannon unbuckled her seatbelt and pulled her work bag over her shoulder. "Since Isabella pointed a finger at him, he might be compelled to say something to defend himself. In that case, we can at least check her story against his."

"If he doesn't lawyer up before he answers anything."

They got out of Dedrick's Impala. Shannon pulled on the front door of The Galway Tap. It was locked.

"You sure he's here?" Dedrick asked.

Shannon knocked on the glass. No one came forward. She shielded her eyes from the mid-day sun and peered into the big window at the front of the restaurant.

"We can always grab lunch and come back," Dedrick said. "I'm sure there's somewhere to eat around here. If you're feeling up to it."

She glared at him. The hangover hadn't gone away quite yet, but that was on a need-to-know basis. "I've felt fine all morning."

"Well, great." He grinned at her from behind the driver's door of his car. "I'm looking forward to getting a couple Blood Marys with you over lunch. There's a place I know."

She marched over to the passenger's door and got into his car. "You think the police union would recommend suspension if I maced a fellow officer?"

"Depends on who it is," Dedrick said.

Shannon smiled at him and batted her eyelashes.

"Well," he said. "The union might not like it if you maced a fellow detective. Probably a couple sergeants who'd want to give you a commendation, though." He started the car. "Take your pick."

They went up North Broadway a couple blocks. Dedrick parked outside of a bar and grill called North End. Inside, the place was stuck in the 1950s. It was dressed in chrome, red vinyl, and black and white tile. They took a spot at a little square table for two with a checkered red and white tablecloth. It was all very wholesome.

Their waitress came to the table immediately. She was somewhere in her late thirties with light hair and tired eyes. She wore a poodle skirt and a little black varsity sweater.

"How are you, Dedrick?"

He flashed that big smile at her. "I'm doing great." He held a hand out toward Shannon. "This is a co-worker of mine, Detective Shannon Rourke."

"Hello," Shannon said.

"Pleased to meet you." The waitress smiled and nodded at her. "What can I get the two of you to drink?"

"A water for me," Dedrick said. "She'll have a Bloody Mary."

Shannon gagged. "Water please," she said. "No ice, lots of lemon."

The waitress smiled. "Lots of lemon. I'll bring you an entire cupful."

"That'd be great." Shannon smiled back.

"Then I'll be right back with your drinks." The waitress smiled at Shannon again. She gave Dedrick a knowing look before she walked toward the kitchen.

On the far side of the restaurant, a computerized juke box played Buddy Holly's "That'll Be The Day." It was just at the part where he belted out the first guitar solo. Dedrick tapped the toe of his dress shoe along with the beat. He hummed the tune to himself while he looked over the menu.

"I didn't think you would've liked a place like this." Shannon opened her menu.

"I like taking my kids here," Dedrick said. "Food's not too bad, either."

The upholstered booths to her left looked like they'd been snatched from a Cadillac Series '62. She pictured him sitting in one with all three of his children bouncing around him and laughing with each other. It almost made her heart melt.

"So, you been feeling okay?" he asked.

"I'm fine, I guess." She kept her eyes on the menu. The grilled chicken salad looked nice and mild. "My stomach hurts a little."

"That all?"

She tilted the menu down to get a better look at him.

"There's nothing else bothering you?" he asked.

"Should there be?"

Dedrick dropped his menu, too. He stretched back in his chair and licked his lips. There was a little grin on his face. "If you don't want to talk about it, I get it," he said. "But I figured maybe you had a couple things you wanted to say. Thought I'd just make myself available to listen."

"About what?"

The waitress came back. "Two waters." She slid their drinks across the table. "And a glass of lemons."

All the while, neither Shannon nor Dedrick broke eye contact with each other.

"Do you two know what you want, or would you like a minute?"

"Grilled chicken salad for me." Shannon stayed locked to Dedrick, trying to get a read on him.

"I'll take my usual." Dedrick looked at the waitress and smiled politely.

"BB King with hot sauce on the side." She wrote down Dedrick's order on her pad. "Next time you see me, I'll have your food."

Dedrick took a sip from his straw. He returned his attention to Shannon.

"Look, I'm not trying to get into your business, Shannon. But if I had a witness come to me and say a choice I made in *my* personal life had had an effect on them," Dedrick said, "I don't know I'd take it as well as you are."

Ah. There it was. This was about what Isabella said— that Colm's murder was caused by a series of events related to Shannon's choice to leave Chicago behind for Stockholm.

"I didn't make him take the money from Ewan. He could've lived here and got clean, the same way Michael did." She took the straw out of her glass, then squeezed and dropped a lemon into the water. "He was teaching Colm how to get by, and at least Colm had the benefit of that. Michael didn't have anybody to help him get through his twelve-step program."

"Then why go to Stockholm?" Dedrick glanced up at her only briefly, like he was scared to ask the question.

"Because as long as we stay in Chicago," Shannon said, "Michael is at risk. I don't want to leave, but it's too easy for him to fall into his old life, and if he does, he's going to start using drugs again. I can't allow that to happen."

"And that's a certainty?"

Shannon grimaced. Dedrick couldn't possibly understand the power that an addiction has over an addict. At least Shannon had an idea, because she'd seen it first-hand. "I know it's hard to understand, but Michael's well-being comes before everything," she said. "After the way we grew up, I owe him that. The best thing I can do for him is to get him out of Chicago, out of this country, as far away from all his troubles as I can."

"If he's the one with all the troubles, why does that mean you have to leave?"

"He's my brother."

Dedrick sighed. He tilted his head back and rubbed his neck.

"What?" Shannon asked.

He brought his eyes back to bear on her. For some reason, they caught her off-guard, and she felt warmth and the gnawing sensation of excitement sneak into her again.

"I thought moving my family up here from Nashville would fix my marriage," he said. "Turns out cheating on somebody still hurts even after you've left it in another zip code. I couldn't run from my problems. I don't think you or your brother can, either."

Shannon had to stop herself from asking why anyone would cheat on Dedrick. He was a good-looking guy, intelligent, funny, and he cared about his kids. What woman would mess that up? But a noticeable silence blocked out the space between them—maybe the first she'd ever felt in Dedrick's company.

The jukebox playing Ritchie Valens' "We Belong Together" didn't help dissolve it.

"You think I should stay?"

Dedrick gave her a tired smile.

The door to the kitchen swung open. Their waitress came straight toward them with a plate in each hand

"One BB King with hot sauce." She put a pulled-pork sandwich with a side of chips and a pickle in front of Dedrick. "And one grilled chicken garden salad." She slid that down in front of Shannon. "If the two of you need anything else, I'll be floating around here," she said. "Just flag me down."

"You know I will." Dedrick politely smiled at her, then set to eating his food.

He and Shannon finished lunch without another word passing between them.

CHAPTER 20

After a couple hours of quiet contemplation in the park while waiting for Afonso Arroz, Michael had come to terms with his situation. He waited on a known criminal. A man who, by Miss Honey's telling, had killed before. A man whom Michael had purposefully angered.

Sitting on this gray and splintered park bench wasn't a terrible way to die, Michael decided.

Maybe it was a poor choice for someone respectable, but not for him. He'd come up against at least a half-dozen different ways to die in his short thirty-five years of life—some self-inflicted, some not. If Afonso decided to shoot him before either of them got word one out, that was fine. Certainly, it ranked better than being mauled to death by Dave McCready's starved pit bulls.

Nobody would really miss Michael anyway. Shannon, maybe. But in time, she'd see that she could do without his mess—she'd carted that load around long enough.

But he didn't think Afonso was the type to shoot him on sight. If all his time working for Ewan taught Michael one thing, it was that guys who'd rose to Afonso Arroz's level were measured. They knew how to walk the fine line between killing and staying their hand just long enough to figure out what somebody like Michael was about.

At least, that's what Michael told himself as he saw Afonso walk across 44th Street and enter the park.

Some guys were psychos. Simple as that.

He thumbed the Taurus Judge in the pocket of his jeans. Michael had five triple-aught shells to fall back on, if nothing else.

"A deep dish, huh?" Afonso smiled as he approached. "You a funny dude."

"I don't know where it comes from," Michael said. "I get caught up in the moment, I suppose."

"My boy Queso probably ain't too happy about how caught up you got," Afonso said. "Dude called me on the way to the ER, said you come out and blasted his kneecap before he got a chance to say wassup."

"Queso? You're funnier than I am—the best nickname I had for him was 'Fat.'"

Afonso sneered. "I ain't come here to talk about jokes, man."

"I'm not here to waste time, either," Michael said. "So, tell me what you know about Colm Keane."

Afonso looked at Michael like he was some kind of moron—like he didn't know exactly what he'd walked into. Maybe the kid wasn't as sharp as Michael thought.

"See, you got it all wrong, man," Afonso said. "You don't get to ask me questions. You get to apologize to me. That's what I need to hear right now—that's the only reason I ain't blow your head off yet."

He hadn't killed Michael because he wanted an apology first? If that was all that kept him alive, why apologize?

"You also don't know where I hid your stash," Michael said.

"Yeah, that might have some play in it," Afonso said. "But straight up, man, I ain't like how you come into my neighborhood and shoot my people. Then you want a sit-down like I owe you something?"

"You don't owe me anything," Michael said. "I'm the one who owes you an apology, your stash, and two grand."

Afonso smirked at him. By the look on his face, it was easy to see he couldn't believe what he was hearing.

"You're playing that hand pretty hard," Afonso said. "I might take the loss just to put a couple holes in your knees before I put one in your head—an eye for an eye, you know?"

"Ewan Keane wouldn't appreciate that."

Afonso's expression dropped. It was almost worth Michael's trouble to see how quickly that predatory smirk on Afonso's face turned to pure terror when he heard Ewan's name. He knew who Ewan was—and he should, if he'd decided to let Colm near his sister—for his own good, if not for hers.

"Don't lie to me, man," Afonso said. "You don't know that dude."

"I assure you I wouldn't lie about who I know."

"If you thought it'd keep me from killing you, you'd tell me how tight you are with Obama."

"There's no need for violence here," Michael said. "I've only come to ask a couple questions."

"Yeah. Tell that to Queso."

Michael knew he'd end up dead right where he sat if Afonso didn't believe he worked for Ewan Keane.

He squeezed the grip of the handgun in his pocket. Michael crossed his legs at the ankles to ensure its muzzle pointed directly at Afonso. If he had to fire from inside his pocket, he'd burn the skin off his own leg and probably get brushed by a couple pellets.

Fair trade. He wasn't about to let Afonso kill him for free.

"Do you think I'd be here talking to you about Mr. Keane's son if I didn't work for him? Why would I stick my neck out for someone who wasn't paying me for my trouble?"

Michael leveled his eyes on Afonso, trying to impart the grave seriousness of what he said to him.

"You think nobody on my side knows your sister, Isabella, is pregnant with Mr. Keane's grandchild?"

Afonso smiled at Michael like he'd been caught in a bluff of his own. "You Irish pricks think you can come across town and dig in anybody's business."

He'd bought the lie. Michael's hand relaxed around his pistol.

"Only our own," Michael said. "Look, Afonso—I don't care about your money or your drugs or whatever else it is you do in that house. And I'm sorry I had to hurt your friend. All I came here to do was find out what you know about Colm's activities."

"Your boss ain't know?" Afonso said. "Ain't that what your people get together about?"

"Mr. Keane doesn't know." Michael lowered his voice like he was spilling a secret. "And he thought, seeing as his son was with your sister, and you are the man you are on this side of town, you might have a little information to share."

"Look man, I don't know nothing about what Colm was into," he said. "I figured whatever game he was running, he was doing it with y'all's blessing, so I let it be. Unlike some around here, I don't put myself into other people's business."

Michael cracked a smile at him. "So you don't know anything about Colm?"

"No, man. I mind my own, and he ain't one of them."

"What about your sister? Would she know something?"

Afonso looked down at the ground. His eyes shifted over to a maple tree's branches shimmying in the hot June wind. "She ain't know nothing—and if nobody wants trouble, you'd be smart to remember that."

That was a lie. Even without Afonso's obvious tell, Michael knew that was a lie. What wife or girlfriend or mistress didn't know what her man was into? It wasn't like Colm had the tightest lips of anybody in Chicago.

"Now, I'd buy that about you," Michael said, "but I know Isabella knew something about Colm's activities."

Afonso shook his head.

"Don't lie to me," Michael said. "You know how many years I've been doing this job?"

"Do I care?" Afonso asked. "I said she ain't know nothing, and that means she ain't know nothing. Leave my sister out of this. She's a civilian, man. That's the last time I'm saying that."

Michael stared at him for a moment. He wanted Afonso to feel the pressure of his gaze on him, to see if the lie would buckle under it. It did. And that was all of the lie

Michael needed to know. If he pressed any harder, he might end up with a bullet in his head.

"Okay," he said. "But if I don't find something about Colm's dealings, I'm going to come knocking on your door."

"You best not come alone," Afonso said. "You ain't catching us sleeping twice."

Michael shook his head. "You know I'm trying to help you, right?"

"Man, whatever," Afonso said. "You over here hassling me. That's all I know."

"Don't you care that your unborn niece or nephew won't ever know their father?"

"Ain't like there's nothing I can do about that now."

"You can help me catch whoever did it," Michael said. "Let me deal with him the way he needs to be dealt with."

Afonso shrugged.

The guy's absolute indifference toward the whole thing struck Michael as bizarre. If he were in the same position as Afonso, there was no way he'd stand in the middle of a park with his hands in his pockets, going about his day like nothing was wrong.

"You think your sister is okay with letting her boy-friend's killer go?" he asked. "You think she'd want to see justice put on the guy who shot Colm?"

"Colm got what he got."

"So, Colm's dead and that's that, then? I thought you at least had some heart in you."

That woke Afonso up. He stomped toward Michael.

For a split second, Michael entertained the idea of letting the Judge go to work, but he thought better of it when Afonso didn't make any move toward grabbing a weapon of his own. Maybe he really did come here unarmed, silly as that was.

"I got *heart*, man." Afonso beat his fist on his own chest. "I'm doing what I'm doing out here to take care of my people—Isabella before all the rest of them."

Michael stared at him.

"Don't you come down here and tell me I ain't got no heart," he said. "I care about my sister's baby. That's why I ain't sad to see Colm go."

"Is that right?" Now they were getting somewhere.

"Yeah that's right!" Afonso practically foamed at the mouth. "I came home more than one time seeing bruises on her—seeing the way he talked to her, and how he treated her. It *killed* me. I'm a man, I gotta protect my sister—my family—but I gotta let all that mess slide because Colm's mobbed up. I can't do nothing about that dude without getting me and mine killed for it." He paused for a second and took a breath. "I didn't know nothing about why Colm got shot or who did it, but how would you feel if you were me?"

There was no doubt in Michael's mind what he'd do if Shannon had a boyfriend rough her up. If the boyfriend had a small army of murderers willing to kill whoever dared put a hand on him, Michael would probably stay the hell out of it, too. And if someone else took care of it for him, he wouldn't shed a tear over it.

"You don't last too long in this business if you play against long odds," Michael said.

"That's why I left the dude alone," Afonso said. "I ain't mad to see him get what he got, but I ain't stupid enough to do it myself."

That was all Michael needed to hear. He jerked his head over his left shoulder. "Your stash is up in the branches of that maple tree."

He got up from the bench and walked toward the south end of the park—away from Afonso and the house on the corner of 44th and Wood.

"Tell Mr. Keane I'll take care of his grandbaby," Afonso said. "He ain't got to worry about that."

Michael kept walking.

CHAPTER 21

After lunch, Dedrick and Shannon walked out to the car in silence.

It looked like it'd continue that way until Dedrick turned the key to start the engine and opened his mouth.

"What I said in there, Shannon—" He stopped himself. "You probably don't want me in your business, but I don't want you to make the same mistake I made."

"I know," she said. She played with her star hooked to her belt—anything to keep her eyes away from him.

Out in the periphery of her vision, she noticed him smiling. He put the Impala in reverse, then pointed the car south on Broadway, in the direction of Ewan Keane's office at The Galway Tap. They were on their way.

"Things got a little too intense, didn't they?" he asked.

"A little." Shannon snorted. "I didn't know whether you'd flip the table over or kiss me."

Oops. She looked out the window. She'd said a couple words too many.

"I was going to do both, but then our food came."
There was a smirk in his voice.

She refrained from commenting. Shannon grabbed her
work bag off the floor. She pulled the zipper back so hard,
she almost ripped it off the teeth. Within a second, she
had her notebook out, and tried to skim over the things
she'd written down. It was a poor attempt to push any
unprofessional thoughts out of her mind.

"Shannon," Dedrick said.

She kept her eyes on her notes.

"Hey, Shannon." He tapped her arm.

Goosebumps prickled up on her elbow. "I'm trying
to brush up on my notes, Detective Halman," she said,
keeping her eyes down.

"Would you cut the awkwardness for a second and
look up?" he half-yelled.

"I'm not being awk—" She looked up.

The Galway Tap was about thirty feet ahead on the left
side of the road. There was glass all over the sidewalk.
The front door had been smashed in.

Dedrick hit the lights on his car and floored it. Shannon
grabbed the radio mic.

"This is unit 411 to dispatch."

"Go ahead, 411," the dispatcher said.

"I need a unit at 3130 North Broadway to help with a
possible 31 in progress."

"I hear you, 411," another officer said. "I'm in the area
and en route to your 31 now."

Dedrick stomped on the breaks. The Impala skidded to
a stop in the middle of the street, lights flashing. Shannon
jumped out of the car as quick as she could. Her heart
pounded ten beats a second, but she kept her cool. She

drew her Glock 40, sure to keep it pointed to the ground and her finger off the trigger.

She ducked between two cars parked at the curb out front of The Galway Tap and pressed herself against a small section of brick wall to the left side of the shattered door. There were bits of glass everywhere, but no blood, and nothing like a brick or a stone used to break the window lay nearby.

For a moment, Shannon felt the Mesopotamian sun scratching at her skin. She smelled cordite and diesel. In her mind's eye, she saw the dashboard of her Marine Corps truck lying against the ground. She saw all the glittering pieces of glass from one of the truck's windows piled on the roof.

She was upside down. The truck had been flipped, and her leg had been mangled.

The memory disintegrated when Dedrick ran up, and leaned into the wall on the opposite side of The Galway Tap's front door.

She nodded at him, then ducked in through the broken pane of glass.

"Chicago PD!" she yelled. She stood up and leveled her weapon. No one answered.

It took a moment for her eyes to adjust to the darkened inside of the bar. The chairs were upturned on the table-tops, and all the TVs were off.

"Looks like no one's home," Dedrick said.

A crash came from the back of the building. It sounded like someone dropped a pan in the kitchen. Shannon's heart butted against the backside of her ribcage.

Both detectives crept toward the noise.

There were likely two entrances to the kitchen. Shannon noted a door behind the bar. Probably another down a hallway to the left, which appeared to lead to the back of the building.

She looked at Dedrick and tilted her head toward the door at the bar. He nodded and went down the hallway.

She carefully approached a hinged part of the bar—it could be that whomever broke that window was crouched on the other side of it, waiting for her. Maybe they had a knife or a shotgun, or had taken a manager hostage....

Shannon blinked her eyes, trying to knock all the scenarios out of her head. She had to focus. Short as she was, Shannon had to step onto the bottom rungs of a barstool to see the back side of the bar.

No one there.

She lifted the hinged surface of the bar and hunched low, making her way toward the kitchen. She had to stop herself from retching when a whiff of beer entered her nose.

A marked car screeched to a stop out front. It briefly grabbed her attention. A pair of uniformed officers left the car's lights on, and sprinted toward the broken front door.

When the first one made his way in, Shannon snapped her fingers and waved her free arm, getting his attention.

She motioned for him to go outside and check the back of the building. It took a moment for him to understand, but finally he nodded, whispered it to his partner, and the two of them sprinted past the big front window of The Galway Tap.

A man's anguished grunt pulled Shannon's mind back to the kitchen.

She walked up to the door behind the bar and peered through a circular window in it. There was blood on the floor—a long streak of it. She couldn't see who made all the noise inside.

There was no time to waste. She backed off from the door. She tensed her face, took a deep breath through her nose, then, with every bit of strength she had in her leg, she sent her right foot flying at the door.

It swung open and crashed into the wall to the right of it.

"Chicago PD!" Shannon ran through the door, pointing her weapon.

Ewan Keane glared at her over his shoulder. Blood ran all the way down the left sleeve of his white shirt. He hunched over the sink, the tap on full blast.

"Hands up!" Dedrick came through the back door.

"It's all right, Dedrick." Shannon lowered her weapon. "We're too late. It's already done."

Robbie Simmons' dead body lay in a pool of blood on the floor.

CHAPTER 22

"I have to admit, you couldn't have arrived at a better time," Ewan said. "If I were a superstitious man, I'd say it was kismet when we made today's appointment together last night."

"Whose weapon is that?" Shannon pointed toward a Colt 1911 on the ground near Robbie. At the same time, an officer dropped a numbered yellow card next to it, marking it as evidence.

"You know I'd hate to insult your intelligence," Ewan said, "but he's the one stabbed. I'm the one shot."

He hunched over the big stainless steel basin sink next to the dish sterilizer. He rested on his good forearm, holding his wounded left arm over the drain. The faucet ran, helping his blood swirl down.

"How long until the EMT arrives?" Ewan asked.

"Ten or fifteen minutes." Shannon looked at the bloody rag they'd used to wrap Ewan's arm until the ambulance made it to The Galway Tap. It was deep red—totally soaked through.

"That one looks saturated." Shannon grabbed a hand towel from what she assumed was a clean stack sitting on the prep island in the middle of the kitchen. "Let me change it out."

He read her with his eyes for a moment. He looked weary as one of the bums idling around Wrigleyville at night, asking for change. "Aren't you supposed to arrest me?" Ewan asked. "There's a dead man lying on the floor of my kitchen."

She pulled a pair of latex gloves out of her bag and put them on. "Won't be much of an arrest if you bleed to death right in front of me." Shannon pinched the corner of the bloody towel wrapped around his forearm. "May I?"

He tensed his mouth and nodded.

"You're lucky it's still attached after he shot you close-range with a .45," she said. "I've seen worse."

"Is that so?" He winced. "Which side of town?"

"Outside Ramadi." She tried her best to keep her hands steady as she removed the rest of the towel.

"Your tour with the Marines." He stiffened his arm again. "I was under the impression they didn't allow women on the front lines."

"Not as combatants," she said.

The towel finally let go of the bullet wound—and there was no doubt it was a bullet wound. It was big as a half-dollar and trickled blood so deep red, it looked black.

"Your arm looks broken," she said.

"Were you a medic?"

She looked up at him. "Does it matter?"

"Only curious," Ewan said. "If you'd rather not talk about it, I won't take offense."

"Hold this." She put his hand on the clean towel, then fished around in the first aid kit Dedrick had brought in from the back of his car. "I was a truck driver," she said. "I heard that was a dangerous job to have." Shannon found the roll of silk tape. She pulled a strip out and cut it with her teeth. "It was."

Dedrick popped his head in from around the corner leading to the back of the bar. "EMT just radioed, Shannon—they're five minutes out."

His cell phone was to his ear. He'd volunteered to file the report with Sergeant Boyd back in the office, which was just as well with her. She'd rather dress a thousand wounds than file a report over the phone.

"Quicker than you thought," Ewan said to her.

"Looks like you picked a good time of day to get shot."

"Kismet," Ewan said.

With his wound dressed, Shannon set her attention on Robbie Simmons' dead body lying face-down on the ground. One of the officers had covered his body with a sheet, but his right hand—and its rose tattoo—stuck out from beneath it.

"Any idea why he shot you in the arm?"

"Because I knocked him around before he had a chance to shoot me in the head," Ewan said. "And to answer your follow-up question, Detective—no, I don't know why he wanted to kill me."

That was doubtful. In any case, she didn't expect Ewan to tell her anything meaningful until she got some kind of leverage on him. She'd just have to poke and prod him until something came out.

"Do you think it had anything to do with Colm's murder?"

He shrugged. "I don't see how."

"Maybe you rubbed someone the wrong way in the past, and now they're coming after your family."

"If I wronged someone that badly, I wouldn't be here talking to you right now. And my son's next-door neighbor wouldn't be here, either."

"So you know who he is."

Ewan nodded. "Robbie. I remember seeing him at the wake yesterday."

"Did you say something to him last night that'd make him want to break down your door and kill you today?"

"I told him 'hello' and 'thank you for coming,'" he said. "I couldn't have spoken to him much beyond that. As I recall, he entered McCullough's with you and your brother, and he left with you two, as well."

True. Robbie didn't seem put off by anything at either point in the night—other than Shannon shooing him away.

"You're sure he didn't act strange toward you in any way?" she asked. "Because if I go talk to someone else, and they give me a different story, you're the first person I'm coming back to with a pair of handcuffs."

"Aren't you supposed to handcuff me now?"

She narrowed her eyes at him.

"Understand that by the time I saw Robbie, I was already a few Scotches into the bottle at my own son's wake," Ewan said. "I may have missed something he'd said or did. My powers of observation weren't as honed as they could have been."

Fair enough.

"Where were you when you heard him break down the door?" Shannon peeled off her bloodied latex gloves and tossed them in the trash. She opened up her work bag and took out her notebook.

"Is this an official questioning?" Ewan asked.

"My notebook?" Shannon titled it outward, where he could see it.

He nodded.

"This is just a pad of paper. It doesn't make anything official. What it *does* do is keep me from relying on my own faulty memory when someone asks me about this case six months from now."

"Why would anyone care about any of this six months in the future?"

Shannon looked up from her notebook, where she'd already begun scratching out notes, and blinked at him. "A man is dead, Mr. Keane. That may be business-as-usual for you, but I take it seriously."

"What exactly do you think I do in a typical day?" He raised his chin and smiled at her. If he were twenty years younger, she'd worry about his charms a little more than she did at this moment.

"Would you mind telling me where you were when you heard Robbie Simmons break through your front door?"

"Back here." He pointed at a pan sitting over a burner on the stove. It held a slice of bread. "I was about to make grilled cheese for lunch, but that plan changed when he showed up. As soon as I heard the glass break, I ran to my office around the corner." He motioned his head toward the door that lead to the small hallway at the back of the restaurant.

"Why?"

"I keep a revolver locked in the safe in my office."

"I assume you have a CFP?" A gun charge might be a good bargaining chip against him for Colm's case.

"Of course," Ewan said. "I keep it, and my FOID, in a safe at home with my other personal documents. I assure you I keep things above-board when it comes to firearm safety—I have my certificate from the mandatory course, if you'd like to see that, too."

"That won't be necessary, Mr. Keane," Shannon said. "Though I'm a bit surprised you keep a weapon here. Boystown is fairly safe, last I checked."

"You never know in this city."

Too true.

She did a quick scan of the kitchen with her eyes. No revolver anywhere to be found.

"If you're wondering where the revolver is, I can assure you I didn't toss it," he said.

"Then where is it?"

"Still in my safe," Ewan said. "I couldn't unlock the door fast enough to get it out before he was on me."

"Would you describe it for me?" She wanted to make sure his story matched up with any and all physical evidence to be found here.

"Sure," he said. "It's nothing special. A bog-standard Smith & Wesson 627 with a wood grip."

She wrote down *S&W 627 revolver in safe* on her notepad. Leaving here without bagging it would be a mistake. "Is it a keyed safe?"

"Yes."

"Would you mind giving me the key?"

"It's hanging in the lock. Probably a little bent. When it occurred to me that Robbie didn't come to chat, I had to turn around and grab him quick as I could." Ewan motioned toward the .45 on the ground. "The only reason we're speaking now is because he didn't have a clear line of sight from the front door of the bar all the way back to my office. He had to get close to me."

"So, he was within arm's reach of you in that little hallway over there," Shannon said. "But he couldn't pull the trigger on you."

Ewan tried to lift his wounded arm, but thought better of it. "He certainly did pull the trigger on me. I tackled him into the hallway a moment after, which was just fast enough to stay alive."

"What happened after that?"

He nodded toward Robbie's body. The sheet came to a point over his neck where it rested on the back end of a knife. It reminded her of some of the tan tents she'd seen at Marine bases in the past.

"I grabbed my letter opener off my desk and defended myself," Ewan said. "I had no intention of killing him. I got him a couple times in the arm with it—probably some good cuts on his hands, too—but I did my level best to run to the bar. There's a loaded 12-gauge behind it. I figured if he saw that, it'd be enough to scare him off."

"But he stopped you here," Shannon said, "in the kitchen."

"The boy lost his mind. I saw him point the gun at me again," Ewan said. "I knew running would've been suicide, so I did the only thing I could—I turned around and fought him with what I had."

He was remarkably cool about the entire thing. That wasn't unexpected from a man who lead a life like Ewan Keane's. Probably wasn't the first time someone had pointed a gun at him, and it probably wasn't the first time he'd stabbed somebody. Admittedly, that was all conjecture on Shannon's part. Ewan didn't have much of a record to speak of, and he would be sure to point that out if she ever verbalized her suspicions.

"You're pretty good with a knife," she said. "I don't know many police who'd be able to land a killing blow like that in the heat of a fight."

"I can recommend a good Krav Maga instructor to the department," Ewan said. "I'd be happy to pay him to come out. As far as I'm concerned, his teachings just earned him much more business from me."

"That's very kind of you," she said. "I think we'll manage without."

Ewan looked at the sheet covering Robbie and shook his head. "I don't know why that boy came here," he said. "I never wished him any harm."

"The paramedic is here." Dedrick entered through the swinging door leading to the bar. "They asked if they should come back to the kitchen, but I told them Mr. Keane can probably walk himself out. I figured the fewer feet we have in our crime scene, the better."

"Agreed," Ewan said. He took a tentative step from the sink. He would have tripped, had Shannon not been close enough to catch him before he fell. Though, calling it "catching" was generous. He had a hundred pounds on her, easily, and it was more like she blocked him from face-planting.

"I got him, Shannon." Dedrick took Keane's arm from around her shoulders then helped him toward the door.

"Thanks," she said. "I'm going to have a look around for a minute and check out Mr. Keane's story."

"Shannon, there are security recordings in my office," Ewan said. "Everything from the last forty-eight hours is sitting in a folder on my computer's desktop."

"I'll take a look at it," she said. "I have more questions to ask you when the paramedic is finished."

"Yes," he said. "We never spoke about Colm."

Ewan and Dedrick hobbled off together.

CHAPTER 23

When the door swung shut behind Ewan and Dedrick, Shannon turned her attention to Robbie Simmons' body beneath the sheet. His last act on Earth had been to make Colm's case ten times more complicated than it already was. Why in the hell would CTA mechanic Robbie Simmons want to kill Ewan Keane?

She put on another pair of latex gloves, then pulled the sheet off him, wadded it up, and threw it on the counter. She went through his pockets. He had the usual—keys, wallet, and phone.

She dropped the keys in an evidence bag. Nothing too exciting there, unless she wanted to take his Chevy S10 for a joyride.

Shannon unfolded his brown leather wallet. Using a set of tweezers, she pulled out each debit and credit card, his ID, and exactly thirty-four dollars in cash. There was a Subway punch card stuck in one of the card slots of his wallet. For completion's sake, she tugged at it with the tweezers.

A piece of it ripped off. It was soft as snotty tissue, and the torn paper fibers came off it like cilia. She guessed it had been through the wash a few times.

Shannon tried to turn the wallet inside-out to get at the card better, but it refused to obey. She stuck her fingers into the card's pocket, found the bottom edge, and tore it out. Half the card's printing stuck to the wallet's lining.

The City of Chicago would thank her for her meticulous work in emptying Robbie Simmons' wallet, she was sure. She dropped the Subway card in the evidence baggie with the rest of his cards. A large piece of it flaked off the back.

No. Not a piece of the card—it was a folded piece of paper stuck to it.

Shannon fished it out of the evidence baggie. She brought it over to the stainless-steel counter next to the wadded-up sheet, and using her tweezers, she carefully unfolded the note. The paper's edges wanted to stay together—it had probably been washed, too—but with a little care, perseverance, and some light swearing, she had it spread open on the counter.

Robbie,

You asked me earlier if he knows. He doesn't. He never will. If he ever found out, I know he'd kill both of us and our baby.

We can finish this one last thing. I love you every day, and I know we'll figure out a way to get through this together.

XOXO

It looked old. The ink was faded, the creases had been well-pressed, and the paper had yellowed from sitting in his sweaty pockets. Who wrote it? Was it from Colm's sister, Elizabeth? What "one last thing" would she want Robbie to do? Kill her father? Was she pregnant?

Shannon carefully bagged the note, separate from the other contents of Robbie's wallet, ensuring it stayed flat.

"Anything I can help with, Detective?" The new crime scene tech, Kristof Rud, stood in the door out to the hall. He had his camera bag on his shoulder.

"I need crime scene photos as soon as you can get them," Shannon said. "Also, I want this note tested for fingerprints. I found it in the vic's wallet, and I can't help but feel his attempt to murder Mr. Keane is somehow related to it."

"Wow." He grinned and took the note from her. "Secret love note—that's exciting stuff. Think he wrote it to himself?"

Shannon rolled her eyes. "Rud, I know you're new, so I'll give you a tip," she said. "Don't make jokes around a body."

"Oh," he said. Without another word, he left the kitchen through the same door he entered.

What the hell was up with that kid?

"Oh," Shannon said mockingly. She shook her head and grabbed Robbie's cell phone.

She swiped the phone's screen. To her surprise, it unlocked—no passcode required. She wasn't used to lucky breaks. At least not in this case. She half-assumed this was a trap and the phone would blow up in her hand.

When it didn't, she went to its call logs. Robbie's last call was made at 10:32 AM, or about two hours ago, to

Pizza Hut. Good idea—murder was probably harder on an empty stomach.

Further down in his logs, it looks like he made and received another pair of calls ... to and from Pizza Hut. At 8:27 AM and 8:43 AM, respectively.

She scrolled through his call logs some more. There was a call made to his work at 5:12 this morning. She jotted the number down. There was a call made to his mom last night before the wake.

And then, the night before that—the night of Colm's murder—there was another call to Pizza Hut at 3:43 AM. Then he missed calls from Pizza Hut at 4:12 and 4:37, until he finally caught a call at 4:52 that lasted half an hour.

Half an hour. With Pizza Hut.

She jotted the number down in her notebook. She'd call when she got back to the station and set up some recording equipment. Worst case scenario, Robbie's best friend worked there, and she'd have to hang up on some pimply pizza boy.

She closed his call log and opened his photos. There were selfies. Too many selfies. Selfies in front of the mirror in his rancid bathroom, selfies from a bench press at a local gym, selfies tinted with green and purple neon lights at a night club, selfies of he and Colm and a few other people all crowded together on a pontoon boat on what Shannon assumed was Lake Michigan.

Selfies, selfies, selfies.

Thank God Shannon had been spared the affliction of her generation.

She was three dozen photos deep into Robbie's selfie diary when the phone vibrated in her hand.

Pizza Hut was on the other end.

Shannon answered the call.

She put the phone near her ear and held her breath. She listened. She didn't dare speak, for fear that whoever was on the other end would immediately realize it wasn't Robbie and hang up.

But whomever called kept quiet, too.

Shannon thought she heard some kind of background noise—but it was indistinct against the humming of the walk-in freezer's compressor to her left. She plugged her ear opposite the phone and tried to pick out what it was she heard. Was it a TV?

No. It was a woman. Was she breathing? Sobbing? Laughing from a distance away maybe? Had "Pizza Hut" called Robbie's phone by accident? Or had whomever it was that dialed his number known what he was up to? Was this woman expecting an update from him about Ewan Keane's death?

The line disconnected.

"You got anything else you need me to take, Detective?" Rud stood in the doorway.

She jumped at the sound of his voice. His eyes cheated down to Robbie's phone in Shannon's hand.

There was more to be had from this little device. She knew something in here would explain why Robbie Simmons tried to murder Ewan Keane.

But she wouldn't find it yet.

She dropped the phone in another evidence bag and sealed it shut. "I want you to keep an eye on this phone," she said. "If it rings, if someone texts it, if the battery runs out—you let the sergeant down in the evidence locker know that I'm to be contacted as quickly as possible."

"Yes, ma'am." Rud took the phone from her

"Rud, before you go—" she grabbed his sleeve "—I want you to run any .45 casings you find here against the casings we picked up at Colm Keane's murder—that murder outside the liquor store near 46th and Ashland."

"I'll schedule the test when I get back to the station," he said.

"Good."

Rud had to sidestep Dedrick on his way out.

"He's running pretty tight this afternoon, isn't he?" Dedrick asked.

"We had a chat."

"Without me?"

She sighed.

"I just wanted to tell you the paramedics are done with Ewan. They're saying they have to take him into surgery at Lakeshore."

"Now?" She couldn't believe it.

"They're loading him into the back of the ambulance."

Shannon jumped to her feet and ran for the front door. More officers and an assistant from the coroner's office milled around the front half of The Galway Tap. She jogged past them, tripping on a chair leg, but catching herself against the wall.

Through the front door, she saw Ewan lying on a stretcher, halfway loaded into the ambulance by the EMTs.

"Wait!" she yelled.

One of the EMTs looked at her, but they continued pushing the stretcher into the back of the ambulance.

Couldn't they hold off for a few seconds? Sure, Ewan had been shot, but he was fine.

She ran into the street, which had been blocked off by squad cars by now. "I said wait!"

They had Ewan loaded up. The nearest EMT turned around. "We can't stop in the middle of putting this man in the back of the ambulance," he said. "We weren't going to drive off before you got here, Detective."

"Thank you." She dropped her hands to her knees and huffed for air. Was she really this out of shape?

She forced herself to straighten out, then rested her hands on her hips.

"Did you know that Robbie dated your daughter, Elizabeth?" she asked.

"He made an attempt," Ewan said, "but he didn't. Elizabeth hasn't dated anyone since—" He stopped.

"Since when, Mr. Keane?"

He had a sorry look on his face—like he was already apologizing in his head for what he was about to say. "Since Michael."

Sure. Elizabeth hadn't dated anyone for seven years. Any woman in Chicago who looked like Elizabeth would have to go through a lot of trouble to avoid male attention.

Shannon decided not to press him on it. It was better she didn't break his fantasy for him.

"Did you know Colm took money from you?" Shannon finally got to ask him the question she'd intended to ask him hours ago.

"Somewhere around eighty thousand, yes," he said. He sounded positively cool about it.

"You knew?"

"Of course I did," he said. "I didn't get where I am by not paying attention to where my money went."

"Why didn't you come to the police about it?"

He made a face like she'd just asked the most ridiculous question he'd heard all day. "No." He snorted. "Why would I report my own son to the police? I knew he had the money, and that was well enough for me."

Well enough for me. Yes, why would Ewan go to the police? That would only make it harder for him to have Colm killed.

"If you'd like to know exactly when and how he took the money, there's a security recording on my computer's desktop. The password is stuck to a note under the keyboard—I always have trouble remembering it."

"Thank you, Mr. Keane," she said. "Good luck in surgery. I'll see you when you're out."

"I hope you start calling me Ewan by then. I know Tommy told you to when you were a little girl."

Her father had told her that, yes—and that's why she never would.

One of the EMTs closed the back door to the ambulance from the inside. It took off right away. A CPD squad car tailed it. The officer driving it would make sure Ewan Keane stayed in his hospital room.

All the better for Shannon—it'd make it that much easier to arrest him for murdering his own son.

CHAPTER 24

Before Shannon viewed the footage of Colm stealing from his father, she checked the security system for video of the fight between Ewan and Robbie.

Through the recorded footage, Shannon saw Robbie pistol-whip the lower pane of glass in The Galway Tap's front door until it shattered. When it did, he came rushing through it. The .45's muzzle was a dowsing rod, guiding him straight back to Ewan's office.

The fight played out almost exactly as Shannon had pictured it in her mind. The multi-angle screen—a composite of the six security cameras in The Galway Tap—showed Ewan abandoning his grilled cheese sandwich and running for his office at the first sound of the door being broken.

He fiddled with his safe while Robbie made his way to the back of the restaurant.

A split-second later, the two men met. Ewan tackled Robbie just as the gun in Robbie's hand discharged.

For a man in his mid-sixties, Ewan Keane had plenty of iron in his blood.

She watched the two of them wrestle it out, separate, then reconvene in the kitchen. Ewan charged Robbie, who had the .45 aimed to kill. The gun went off right as the two connected, and the bullet caught Ewan in the arm. The rest of the footage showed Ewan and Robbie wrestling at the foot of the kitchen's center island. There were maybe twenty seconds of the two of them battling on the ground before Ewan got to his feet, leaving a dead Robbie Simmons behind.

Over the next three minutes of video, Ewan stumbled around the kitchen, looking for something to stop up his wound. He found an old towel and wrapped it around his arm. Shortly thereafter, Shannon burst into frame, gun drawn.

She paused the video.

Ewan Keane's desk—a piece of laminate board bolted into supports in the wall—creaked under her as she shifted her weight.

She expected someone with Ewan's wealth to have a more extravagant office space. She expected his office to smell like cedar, to intimidate her with its power and majesty. Something with a panoramic view of Chicago's skyline. He should have a teakwood desk with hand-carved scrollwork up and down the sides. A desk big enough to butcher a cow on.

What Ewan had was a windowless room jammed into the back of The Galway Tap. It shared one wall with the men's bathroom—currently occupied by Kristof Rud playing games on his smartphone (she heard it through the wall). The other wall butted up against the kitchen.

If Shannon laid on the floor, aligning herself along the office's longest dimension, she'd have to bend her knees to fit. The room had probably been a broom closet before it was his office.

His computer was some old piece of junk from the mid-2000s. Only Ewan Keane and the kid on Geek Squad who'd been damned to keep this giant calculator running knew how it had survived this long.

Shannon closed the video playback of the fight. Beneath it, a folder marked "Colm" waited on the computer's desktop.

She opened it. The folder contained another video, dated three days ago. She double-clicked it and while the video loaded, Shannon looked under the desk. The little safe sat in the corner, nestled in the shadows. She grabbed her flashlight out of her work bag and shined it at the safe.

A bent key hung from the lock. Otherwise, the safe looked fine, if not a little old. If Colm had stolen from the safe as Ewan had claimed, he must've had a key.

Out of the corner of her eye, she noticed the security footage start on the computer's screen.

The video's time-stamp read last Wednesday—the night before Colm's murder. The camera pointed directly at the safe, from a corner of Ewan's office near the ceiling. Shannon looked up and to her right. The camera was still there.

Colm entered the frame. Even in the low-resolution footage, she knew the back of his head from all the colorful tattoos creeping up his neck. He dropped to a knee, reached under the desk, and a little piece of silver glinted from his hand. It had to be a key. He pulled the safe's door open.

Out came the money.

Big, fat bricks of it, bound up by rubber bands that looked like they'd snap off if he moved the money too quickly. If it was the supposed amount of eighty thousand dollars, it had to be in small bills. Who kept that kind of petty cash on-hand? It had to be dirty money. Probably why Ewan hadn't reported it.

Maybe Michael knew something about it.

No. She wouldn't put her brother in that position. His sobriety depended on it.

Colm deposited it all into a pillow case at his feet. There was no urgency to his movements, no fear of seeing his father show up and catch him in the act.

Something flashed in the corner of the video's frame. Shannon paused it. She reversed the video and hit play.

There it is again. Just a quick flutter of something pale. Maybe a bug too close to the lens?

She paused the video and did a frame-by-frame step back.

The thing flashed in the corner. Motion blurred it, making it too difficult to see what it was exactly.

One of these frames had to have clearly captured it. She tapped the left arrow key on the keyboard. Once, twice, and on the third time she had no doubt what it was.

It wasn't a bug. It was a hand.

Someone else had been with Colm that night.

She squinted at it. She got her eyes so close to the old 4:3 LCD panel monitor, she saw the individual pixels in the screen.

There was something on the back of the hand. A shirt cuff? Part of a watch? Maybe Colm's accomplice had on gloves?

She stepped the video forward and back a couple times. She didn't think CPD kept a database of the hands of known felons anywhere.

Forward and back. Forward and back.

Then her mouth fell open. It was the rose tattoo on the back of Robbie's hand.

CHAPTER 25

Shannon watched the coroner's assistant stuff the gurney with Robbie Simmons' body into the back of the panel truck. She had a new front-runner for Colm's murder, but why would he have gone after Ewan? Was he afraid of reprisal? Was Robbie afraid that Ewan would find out he'd killed Colm and come after him? Or had Robbie simply wanted to erase anyone who knew about the stolen money?

What about Isabella?

Shannon's phone rang in her pocket. She pulled it out. The screen displayed a picture of Michael; she'd taken it when they'd gone to Mackinac together and he'd accidentally stepped in the biggest pile of horse manure she'd ever seen.

He hadn't been happy about it.

"Hello?"

"Isabella's brother knows something about Colm's murder." Michael sounded out of breath. "He's a player on the south side, Shannon. He's running a crew over here. He had something to do with it, I know he did."

What the hell? Had he figured all that out from looking at Facebook posts?

"I'm not going to ask how you came by that information," she said, "but I *am* going to save you any further trouble and tell you you're wrong."

"I'm right," he said. "I know I am."

"Really?" She looked around to make sure no one was in earshot. "Because I'm sure I just caught the guy who killed Colm," she hissed into the phone.

There was a brief moment of silence. It was broken by a car honking on Michael's end of the phone.

"Where are you?"

"Who killed him?" Michael asked. "Did he say he'd been hired by someone?"

"He didn't say anything. He's dead. Courtesy of your old boss."

She heard another car hum past from his side of the call.

"Ewan." He didn't sound all that surprised. "Did you arrest him?"

"He won't be charged with anything," she said. "It was self-defense. He's over at the hospital being prepped for surgery."

"What happened to him? Is he okay?" He practically shouted into the phone. "Was he shot?"

That was the first time she'd heard Michael get excited about anything in months. Even the Cubs couldn't get him going like they used to.

"He's fine," she said. "He caught a bullet with his forearm. The bone is shattered, I'm sure, but knowing him, he'll come out of it."

Michael exhaled. "Jesus, Shannon, don't scare me like that."

"You're the one calling me with information about my case," she said. "How about we make an agreement that you never do that again?"

What was he doing? Hunting down leads for her? She couldn't believe he'd think that was okay. If he wanted her to figure out who murdered Colm, he had to stay out of it. She couldn't risk Michael's well-being.

"Yeah," he said. "I know I shouldn't have gone looking into it."

That came a little too easily—but she had other things to take care of now.

"I'll see you at home." She hung up.

But what if Michael was right? What if Isabella's brother knew something about Colm's murder?

Why did it matter at this point? Robbie had a clear motive—taking the money he'd stolen with Colm. If the casings from Robbie's 1911 .45 came back as a match to the casings found at Colm's murder, that'd place the murder weapon in Robbie's possession. Murder weapon plus motive equaled conviction.

Shannon would hit the plane to Stockholm with another closed case.

But not a clear conscience.

She saw Dedrick emerge from The Galway Tap.

"I need to borrow your car." Shannon tossed the keys to her Jeep to Dedrick.

He caught them before he even knew they were coming. "What? Why?"

"I have to go talk to Isabella," she said. "She was right about Colm robbing Ewan. But he had help."

"From who?"

"Robbie Simmons."

Dedrick looked at the panel truck from the coroner's office and shook his head. "Think she knew about that?"

"I intend to find out," Shannon said. "That's why I need your keys. You can get a ride to Blue Island from one of the officers. If I'm not back by the end of the day, take my Jeep home."

He reached into his pocket and tossed his keys to her. "Be careful with my baby, Shannon. They don't keep many of those at the motor pool."

"Of course."

The Impala was in the same place they'd left it when she and Dedrick initially entered The Galway Tap after lunch. She walked over to it.

"On second thought, why don't I come along with you?" Dedrick walked toward her.

"Someone has to sew things up here," she said. "I need casings from Robbie's gun and the casings we found at Colm's murder scene compared as soon as possible."

"You think Robbie shot him?"

She opened the driver's door, then eased herself into the seat. "He did it for the money." She closed the door.

The interior of the Impala smelled like Dedrick's cologne. Shannon let herself take a breath of it before she slid the key into the car's ignition.

Dedrick knocked on the window. She jumped in the seat—did he notice her smelling his car? She lowered the window.

"If you think Robbie killed Colm," he said, "doesn't that close the case?"

"We still don't know why Robbie tried to kill Ewan."

"And I'm guessing you intend to ask Isabella about that," Dedrick said.

"For a start," she said. "I think she knows more about her boyfriend's activities than she let on. Or her brother Afonso does."

"What makes you say that?"

Shannon started the car. "Women's intuition." She winked at him and pulled away.

CHAPTER 26

At the stop light before the ramp to get on Lake Shore Drive, Shannon pulled out her phone. She dialed Isabella's number. It rang four times, then went to a generic voicemail box.

The light turned green, but Shannon had her eyes on the phone. She redialed Isabella's number. At the same time, someone honked behind her. People in Chicago had no patience for anything—not even an Impala with CPD license plates.

Isabella answered on the second ring this time.

"I can't talk," she sucked in a tense breath, "right now."

"Isabella? It's Detective Rourke. Is something wrong?"

No answer but Isabella's sobbing.

"Isabella, if you're in trouble, I want to help you," Shannon said.

Isabella tried to say something, but she only huffed and cried. The lack of any answer from her was perhaps the worst answer possible.

She took the ramp onto Lake Shore. As soon as she was on the highway, her foot smashed down on the accelerator.

"Hold on, Isabella, I'll be at your house as quickly as I can."

"No," she said. "No, I'm fine." She heaved another deep breath.

"No, you're not," Shannon said. "Do you need me to call an ambulance?"

Isabella hung up.

Shannon weaved through traffic. She grabbed the radio mic and held it in the same hand she used to hold the steering wheel. Her free hand dipped into her back pocket and pulled out the slip of paper she'd had Isabella write her address and number on.

"This is 411 to dispatch," Shannon said.

"Go ahead, 411."

"I have a female subject, pregnant, residing at 4611 South Marshfield Avenue. I'm en route, and I think there's something wrong."

Shannon dodged a Prius going 5 miles under the speed limit in the left lane. She laid on the horn as she zipped past, then flipped on the car's lights and siren.

"Could you be more specific, 411?" the dispatcher asked.

"No," Shannon barked back. "I don't know what's wrong, but I think she might need medical attention. I need a patrol unit and an ambulance at that address ASAP."

"We'll get someone from the area, 411. Drive safe."

Drive safe. Right.

There was nothing worse than darting to a scene like this. Even with all the lights and sirens in the world strapped to her car, there were enough entitled nuts in Chicago who thought they had the right-of-way in every situation.

Still, she made it down Lake Shore in one piece. She made it down I-90, too, and exited toward Pershing, going past US Cellular Field. The car must've done seventy all the way down to Ashland, where Shannon slowed it to sixty. Halfway down Ashland, she passed AOK King Liquors, where Colm had been shot. She never realized how close Isabella's house was to the murder scene. Had she been there that night?

She turned right onto South 46th street, and slowed up. Isabella's place was a white duplex, about three houses down from the corner.

One of CPD's marked cars was already there. An ambulance was parked right behind it.

Shannon stopped Dedrick's Impala in the middle of the street, threw it in park, and ran out without turning off the engine. She ran to the open back of the ambulance, where a paramedic hung his feet off the tailgate and smoked.

"What are you doing?"

The paramedic shrugged. "You should talk to the officer."

Out front of the house, an officer talked into the radio on her shoulder. "411?"

Shannon flashed her detective's star. "Where's Isabella Arroz?"

"Ma'am, I'm sorry, but for the last five minutes, I've knocked on every door and peeked into every window on this side of the duplex. There's no one home."

Did they have the right address?

"Go knock on the neighbor's door." Shannon pointed to the house to the north. "Ask for Isabella Arroz."

Without a word, the officer turned north and hopped the chainlink fence separating the yards.

Shannon went south. Maybe one of her neighbors saw or heard something.

She bounded up a crooked trio of concrete steps, then knocked on the neighbor's front door.

An old man ripped the door open, scowling. "The hell do you people want?"

"I'm sorry to bother you, sir, but do you know if Isabella Arroz lives next door?" Out of habit, Shannon leaned to her right and tried to look past the old man and into his house.

"Yes, she lives next door," he said. "And when you see her, would you tell her that some people in this neighborhood need to sleep?"

"Did something happen?"

He rolled his eyes. It didn't feel great to be on the other end of that. "It's those damned kids," he said. "They're howling like banshees every time she and her hoodlum brother go out to their car—I don't need to hear the woman herself screaming bloody murder, too."

"She was yelling?"

"Yelling and blubbering like an old lady at a funeral," he said. "I woke up from my nap thinking the whole goddamn world was coming to an end, but it was only them going out to their car."

Well, the crying matched up with what Shannon had heard over the phone.

"Did they indicate where they were going?"

"The hell if I know! I poked my head out the door to tell them to shut up, but they were already speeding down the street," he said. "I don't know why I waste my breath. I don't talk to them, and I don't want to."

"Do you know which way they went?"

He pointed south. "If you're going to arrest them, give that brother of hers a little mace for me. God knows he could use it."

"Thank you. You've been very helpful, sir." Shannon decided to let that little remark slide.

The old man grumbled and slammed the door shut.

Shannon cut across the front yard, back to Isabella's side of the duplex. "Found anything?" she yelled to the officer, who was already two houses down.

"Nobody's home," the officer yelled back.

"That's all right," Shannon said. "Keep knocking until you've been to all these houses." She motioned at the handful of houses across the street. Didn't look like anyone was home there, either, but it was worth knocking, at least.

She walked up the concrete steps in front of Isabella's side of the duplex. From what the old man next door had said, they'd left in a hurry. Maybe she'd get lucky and the door would be left open a crack—it was perfectly legal to pop her head into the house in that case.

Their front door was apple-red, and the paint had chipped off around the doorknob with age. It was also closed tight. Shannon put her hand on the knob and turned, but the deadbolt had been locked.

She sighed and sat on the front edge of the porch. She grabbed her phone out of her pocket.

"Can I go?" the EMT asked from the street. He held up an e-cigarette. "Or should I change out my flavor?"

Behind him, she noticed Dedrick's Impala in the middle of the street, the driver's door hanging open and the engine on. Shannon hopped down from the porch. "I don't think I'm going to need you," she said to the EMT. "Smoke more if you want—I don't care."

He shrugged and grabbed a small glass vial from his pocket. "Cut yourself?" he asked as Shannon walked past.

"What?" She stopped.

"Your hand's bleeding," he said. "Stay here a minute. I'll check it out." He hopped up from the tailgate, e-cigarette hanging from his lips, and rummaged through a drawer nearby.

When did she cut herself? What could she have possibly done it on?

"You know, detective, it's okay to ask me for help when you hurt yourself." The EMT hopped from the back of the ambulance. He took Shannon's right hand and wiped at her palm with an alcohol pad. "Believe it or not, helping people is why I showed up here when the call came in."

"I thought she'd be here." Shannon watched Isabella's house as if it would spew some kind of secret the moment she took her eyes off it. "My witness, that is. I called her and she sounded like she was in trouble. She's pregnant."

"Mhm," the EMT said. He turned her hand over. Then he turned it back. He held her hand up and examined her wrist. "Did that hurt at all?"

"Did what hurt?"

"The alcohol pad. Did you feel anything when I cleaned you off? Because I can't see where you've been cut."

She looked at her hand. She realized she hadn't felt anything because she hadn't been cut.

She took off toward the front door of Isabella's house.

"Detective, you're gonna bleed everywhere!" the EMT said. "Isn't that bad for the crime scene or whatever?"

Shannon stomped up the steps. Reflexively, she grabbed for her work bag, but realized she'd left it in the Impala, so gloves weren't an option at this moment. She crouched and peered at the underside of the doorknob. Blood.

Enough blood that a few drops of it had joined together in a small pool at the foot of the door. How had she missed that?

She got to her hands and knees. She looked across the concrete porch toward the front steps and saw another drop. The porous concrete had almost swallowed it up, but she'd seen enough blood in her time to know it was there. She followed it and saw another on the front walk. Then another and another until the sparse trail ended near splotches of old grease and oil on the driveway.

She remembered the neighbor saying Isabella and her family had gotten into their car.

"What's the nearest hospital to here?" Shannon said to the EMT.

"Mitchell." Knots of thick, white vapor shot out of his mouth when he spoke. "Over on the far side of Washington Park."

"I know where it is." Shannon was already halfway to the Impala. "Can you put in a call to the UC hospital and see if Isabella Arroz has checked in?"

"No." The EMT looked at her like she was crazy. "HIPPA laws."

Fine. She'd go check it out herself. If her hunch was wrong, Isabella probably wasn't leaving whatever hospital she was at anytime soon. There'd be time to check elsewhere.

"Do me a favor," Shannon said. "Tell that officer she doesn't have to knock on anymore doors."

"Isn't that your job?" the EMT asked.

Shannon didn't have time to answer him. She closed the Impala's door and started the engine. She kept the lights on and gunned it toward Bernard Mitchell Hospital.

CHAPTER 27

Shannon's GPS said it'd take her seventeen minutes to get from Isabella Arroz's house to Mitchell Hospital.

She did it in eight—one of the perks of having CPD lights on her car. She would've requisitioned something from the motor pool like Dedrick had with this Impala, but she'd feel like a traitor to her Jeep.

The parking attendant directing traffic into the hospital's front loop tried to stop her as she sped past. With the Impala's red and blues flashing, he should've gotten the point.

She took an emergency parking spot, cut the engine, and jogged into the hospital.

Three women sat at the front desk, chatting amongst themselves. Shannon flashed her star at them. One nodded at her and hit the button to open the double security doors which separated the waiting room from the hospital's emergency department.

A detective's star was good enough to get her through the door, but how far would it really take her? Shannon imagined if she asked any of the nurses buzzing back and forth through the hall beyond the double security doors, they'd balk the same as the EMT had.

Nothing to do but keep walking.

Shannon peeked through any open doorways she happened to come across. Most were empty. Half-comatose patients watching TV from their beds through slitted eyes occupied some others.

No Isabella.

There were probably three dozen rooms in the emergency department of Mitchell Hospital—any one of which Isabella could be in. No one here would look kindly on Shannon if she began knocking on doors.

She'd have to figure out a way to find Isabella discretely.

To her left, Shannon found the answer to her problem— the nurse's station. It was a big, semi-circular counter with a computer on it and lots of official-looking documents in slots behind it.

And it was empty.

Shannon checked left down the hall, then right. Nurses buzzed in and out of rooms in their colorful scrubs, too busy with their patients to worry about what she may or may not be doing.

She practically jumped behind the big counter.

But what was she looking for? Shannon paused for a moment. She had to find something with Isabella's name on it—an insurance card, a room number, or a report.

She shuffled through the papers in the slots. One stack was blank forms for uninsured patients, another was forms for patient allergy information, and a third was a set of instructions on how to do the Heimlich maneuver.

There weren't any paper records here.

Of course Mitchell Hospital didn't keep paper records — it's the twenty-first century. If she were to find any information about where Isabella was, she'd find it through the PC.

It was probably locked. She tapped the space bar. The monitor flicked on. Yep, locked — she needed a username and password to see anything.

She sighed. Maybe if she hung around long enough, she'd catch Isabella's brother coming or going. He wouldn't be hard to recognize, but she'd probably have a hell of a time getting any information out of him. He didn't look like a talker.

Her odds with the computer were better.

Maybe someone left a username and password lying around on a sticky-note or a slip of paper. Shannon felt around the back of the monitor. Nothing but wires and dust. She checked under the big, semi-circle desk. She saw more wires, more dust, and a lone sock — which raised some questions.

She shuffled some papers around on the desk. In an emergency department this large, there had to be someone forgetful or careless with their login information — someone who could never remember their password.

Like Ewan.

Shannon grabbed the keyboard and flipped it over. A teal sticky-note was attached to it. On it, someone had scrawled their information. Username: SBOWLES. Password: 5H4RK4TT4CK.

Easy.

Shannon entered the information and the computer unlocked. A searchable patient database was the first thing she saw. She put in Isabella's name, and the computer did the rest.

Isabella Arroz was in room 132. Shannon's eyes continued to scan down the screen until she saw the words, "premature birth."

Oh, God. Of all things, why did it have to be that? Was this some cruel twist of fate—Shannon Rourke put on a case where a baby's life was in jeopardy?

Pea-soup green walls blocked any other thoughts out of her mind. In her head, she heard that Marine Corps nurse ask why Shannon hadn't told anyone.

Shannon's knees went weak. She blinked and gritted her teeth. The cream-colored walls of Mitchell Hospital came back to her.

She made her way down the hall as casually as she could. None of the nurses seemed to suspect her. A hospital like Mitchell didn't leave time for suspicions.

Room 132 waited ahead and to the right. She knocked on the door before she opened it partway.

"Isabella?" Shannon whispered.

A curtain blocked view of the room's bed. She walked in.

The room was quiet. The lights were on. Some machine beyond the curtain beeped, and she heard the subtle hiss of oxygen.

Shannon slid the curtain aside.

Her throat closed on itself as soon as she saw Isabella.

She laid in the bed, sleeping. Her beautiful hair was spread out along the pillow. It made her appear as if she were in a constant state of falling into place. Tubes and wires came from her body. They plugged into machines next to the bed, machines on the wall, machines on carts, machines on shelves—machines anywhere the hospital staff could stuff them without burying Isabella alive.

There was a chair at the bed's side. Shannon took a seat. She couldn't bring herself to ask Isabella anything. Not now.

Then Isabella stirred in the bed. Tears gathered in the corners of her closed eyes.

Shannon grabbed her hand. "It's okay." She stroked Isabella's hair. "You're in the hospital. Your baby will be okay."

The act leapt beyond anything a police officer should do. Protocol had no place here.

Isabella's eyes fluttered open. She looked at Shannon with pupils as big as quarters. She was drugged out of her mind.

"Hi, baby," Isabella said. She squeezed Shannon's hand. "I'm sorry."

"It's Detective Rourke," Shannon said. "What happened to you?"

Isabella's mouth twisted up in pain. Tears rolled down her cheeks and onto the white hospital pillow.

"We were so close, baby," she said between sobs. "We had the money. We had Windsor. He was gone…. We were so close."

She was delirious. Shannon didn't know what to say. Isabella thought she was Colm.

"You did what I asked—you did great," Isabella said. "You did better than Afonso could have."

Did what she asked? Had it been *her* idea to rob Ewan? Did she know about Robbie's involvement?

"I was so proud of you," Isabella said. "You were a man. You stood up. You protected your family just like you said you were always gonna do." She smiled at Shannon. "You did it right."

Isabella choked on her own sobs for a moment. "I'll miss you," she said.

CHAPTER 28

"Who are you?"

Shannon turned her eyes from Isabella. A doctor stood half-obscured by the curtain blocking the door, his reading glasses focused on her.

"I'm a friend," Shannon said. "I heard from Afonso that Isabella was in the hospital, so I came to see she was okay."

A convincing lie.

"I'm sorry, miss, but this room is open to family members only," the doctor said. "You'll have to leave. Now."

She looked at Isabella.

"Don't leave," she said. "I can't do this alone." Another pair of tears darted down from Isabella's eyes.

Isabella didn't know who she was crying for. And neither did Shannon. She felt a bit like a vulture feeding on Isabella's suffering.

Even if she stayed in the room, if she planted her feet and refused to budge until a pack of security officers came and dragged her away, Shannon wouldn't get any of the closure she craved.

She let go of Isabella's hand, then stood up from her chair. She had a new lead in her case—Isabella probably had had a hand in stealing Ewan's money. That was worth something, wasn't it? Even if she had to prey on a woman at her most vulnerable to get it.

"Is her baby alive?" Shannon asked.

The doctor's expression curdled. "Miss, you need to leave."

"Right," Shannon said. She stepped away from Isabella's bedside and felt like she'd had a ton of bricks dropped on her.

Once out in the hall, Shannon made her way back toward the hospital's front door.

"You!" A security guard approached her just outside of Isabella's room. "I saw you access that computer at the nurse's station."

She didn't have the patience for this. "I'm a cop."

"I don't care who the hell you are. You're coming with me right now." The guy tried to grab her by the wrist. She caught his arm with both hands and twisted it around until she had him lying on his belly in the middle of the hall, crying mercy.

Nurses and patients up and down the hallway gasped, but she didn't pay much mind to them. She held her star up where everyone could see it. A few of them went back to what they were doing, but others stayed quiet and kept their eyes on her.

The security guard groaned wordlessly on the ground.

Shannon looked down at him and something in his face—a twist of his lip, his watering eyes—something touched the humanity in her.

What in the hell did she just do?

She got off him.

Suddenly, she was out front, her hand on the door of Dedrick's Impala, the bile rising up in the back of her throat. She ripped the car's door open, then flung herself into the driver's seat. She leaned up against the steering wheel and cried.

Motherhood came to drown her again.

She was supposed to have bailed herself out of it at the VA a long time ago. She'd used that bucket every day for a year. All the psychologists and the support groups and the volunteers—they had brought buckets for her, too.

When that didn't work, they helped her build a dike. They helped her wall off pain that should've receded a long, long time ago.

But here it came to swallow her up.

Shannon opened her eyes.

She was laid up in that stuffy pea-soup-green recovery room in Germany again. Her right leg had been shattered after the IED flipped her truck. The surgeons had managed to fix it, and now it hung from a sling over her hospital bed.

"Lance Corporal Rourke." That blond Marine Corps nurse stood in the door to Shannon's room. She had a green file folder clutched to her chest. She sighed and grimaced at Shannon. "Why didn't you tell anyone?"

"Tell anyone what?"

Shannon wiped the tears from her eyes. She was back in the Impala, free from the worst part of her intrusive memory.

There would be times when things like this happened. She remembered what the psychologist at the VA told her: she had to have a strategy. She needed to come up with a way to bail herself out again at a moment's notice. She did, but Frank wasn't here. He was probably at home, lying in her bed. Her fingers twitched as if they could break the space between her and her dog, and scratch the loose folds of skin over his shoulders.

Breathe. She should breathe. She huffed air in through her nose, then blew it out of her mouth. In through the nose, out through the mouth. In and out and in and out.

Her phone rang. It was Michael.

She sucked up the tears, took a breath, and swiped the screen of her phone to answer the call. "Hi," she said, sounding altogether unconvincing.

"Shannon?" he asked. "What's wrong?"

"I'm at the hospital."

"What? Are you hurt?"

"No, I'm fine," she said. "I just—I need to come home. I'm tired. I've worked too long today."

"Okay," Michael said. "I'm nearly there, but I can come get you. Where are you?"

"Mitchell Hospital," she said. "But I'll be fine to drive. I'll see you at home."

She hung up. She looked at herself in the rear-view mirror. Her eyes were bloodshot and ringed with red. Strands of her dark hair had come out of her ponytail and hung down over her forehead. Her cheeks were flushed, like she'd come in from shoveling up snow after one of the blizzards came roaring over the lakes.

This was no way for a Marine to be. No way for a CPD detective to act.

Shannon took a deep breath through her nose and turned the ignition on the Impala.

When she got home and got to hold Frank, everything would be okay. She'd have to make it on her own until then.

CHAPTER 29

Shannon drove Dedrick's Impala all the way back to the curb in front of her apartment. He wouldn't be happy about leaving his take-home car with her all night. She'd call him later and apologize, but for now, she just had to get out of the scouring outside world and into her place.

In the brief seconds it took to get from the car to the front door of her building, Shannon heard music and singing slip through the evening haze over Wrigleyville. The seventh-inning stretch over at the Cubs game was about halfway through. People would be spilling out of the stadium and into the bars soon.

While they did, she'd be curled up next to Frank, music from her headphones blasting away the bad memories.

The old door at her apartment building's entrance creaked open. She took the steps up and unlocked the door to her place.

Frank was right there on the other side. He looked up at her with big brown eyes, like he could smell the grief on her. His tail swished left and right with excitement. His tongue sneaked little glimpses of her from between his big, saggy lips.

She started to feel better already.

"Hey, buddy!" She dropped to her knees and hugged him. She squeezed him so tight he groaned, but he didn't shy away from her. He pressed into her harder, almost knocking her over. His tail pounded against the door-frame—*thud, thud, thud.*

Frank licked her face. This big, dumb dog wanted nothing more than to see her, to be next to her, and to feel her hands scratching and rubbing him. Well, all that and the occasional walk. She felt tears fighting to make their way out of her again, but she held them back.

"All right, buddy, let me inside." She stood up and stepped past him and into her apartment. She closed the door behind her.

"Hi." Michael's voice came from the kitchen. She couldn't see him. "You hungry?"

"I'm starving." She hadn't touched anything since her grilled chicken salad nearly eight hours ago. She almost laughed when she thought of Dedrick and his kids in that chintzy diner together.

"Take a seat, then," Michael said. "I'm almost ready to plate dinner."

She pulled a chair out at their little circular dinette table and collapsed into it. Behind her, she heard Michael click the stove off and scrape something out of a frying pan.

Frank, who thought himself to be the size of a teacup poodle, squeezed under the table. His tail whacked her on the thigh.

She reached down and rubbed her knuckles on his ear. Frank couldn't stop himself from pressing harder against her hand, to the point that she was almost pulling wax out of his ear canal.

"How was the drive home?" Michael asked. "Feeling any better?"

"I am now," Shannon said to Frank.

"I want to talk to you about our conversation earlier," Michael said.

Shannon didn't know what there was to talk about. He couldn't go hunting for information about Colm and that was that.

"I'm sorry I stuck my nose into your job," he said. "You were right. I shouldn't have done that. I just had to know how Colm had come by his money."

She sighed. In all the commotion, she hadn't mentioned anything to Michael about Colm's plan to go to Canada, and why. She'd have to tell him sooner or later. But how could Shannon tell her brother something she was certain would unstitch him?

"It's all right," she said.

"I just couldn't quit wondering about him," Michael said. "Me and Colm, we just—I gotta know what happened to him. Good or bad."

"There's something you need to hear."

He sat a plate of salmon and sautéed asparagus in front of her, and a similar plate across the table for him, then he took his seat. "Okay."

She stared at the fish. He knew exactly what she liked. He deserved better family than her.

"Michael, Colm was—"

When her eyes met him, she had to stop. There was something wrong with the way he looked. It wasn't just that he was disheveled and tired, but he looked ... not himself.

"Is something wrong?" he asked.

"What have you been doing today?"

"You go first." He forked a piece of salmon. Whatever it was—and she was sure it was something—he didn't want to talk about it.

"Michael, what the hell happened to you?"

He shrugged. "I'm fine."

"Did you ... you didn't—"

Silence. His face went from tired to defensive in a matter of seconds.

"What?" he snapped. "Did I what?"

"You didn't *use*, did you?"

Another uncomfortable pause—the tension was strong enough to make Frank's hackles come to attention on his shoulders.

"Did I use heroin today, Shannon?" Michael said. "Is that what you want to ask me?"

Words escaped her. She didn't want to say it, but he looked like he had. There was a shine to his eyes—a certain quality they lost when he used. They looked back at her from across the table, dull as a stone.

"Did you?"

"No. I didn't."

His answer didn't make her relax.

He tore another piece of his salmon with his fork, then stuffed it in his mouth.

God. What had she become? His mother? Just because he looked a little rough, it didn't mean he was back on heroin. She had to trust he wouldn't do that.

"I'm sorry," she said into her plate. "It wasn't right for me to accuse you."

The tears came out again.

"Shannon?" Michael's fork clanged against the dish. "Shannon, it's fine."

"It's not." She shook her head. "None of this is fine."

"I'm not upset," Michael said. "I don't blame you for being suspicious."

"Colm wanted money to move to Canada," she blurted. "He and a friend robbed Ewan to get it."

Michael sat back in his chair. He took the news a lot better than she expected. Maybe he didn't understand the reason why Colm wanted to move.

But her brother wasn't that dumb.

"I figured he'd try to get out of the country," Michael said. "He'd told me before that he didn't want to stay in Chicago."

"I can't blame him," Shannon said. "I don't want to stay here either. I'm tired of all the baggage—of being the daughter of a mobster, of a man who killed himself. I see Tommy every time I look at the streets. I see him with a belt in his hand chasing after you when we were kids. I see him scowling at the wall with a pile of empty beer cans next to him, while mom did nothing but turn see-through. To me, all of Chicago is Tommy. The wind smells like the booze on his breath, and the buildings look gray as his hateful eyes, and I see all the anger he put into you, Michael."

Shannon had seen it a thousand times in her cases. File after file of young men and women never loved by those who were supposed to love them, nursed on a steady diet of indifference, left to rot through their lives.

As people grew, that rot spread. Not only within themselves, but without. They turned to anger, they turned to violence, they turned to destroying anything they could.

They killed each other. They killed themselves. They killed anyone who was handy.

"This city can be terrible—I know. I was part of it." Michael clenched his jaw. "But if I learned anything about life at my meetings, it's that running away from trouble is worse than the trouble itself."

And what was Stockholm to her, if not a place to run away from her troubles? She thought back to what Dedrick had said in the diner.

Suddenly, her food was a lot less appetizing.

"I think I need a shower," she said.

Shannon excused herself from the table and made her way to the bathroom. Frank followed.

She closed the door behind her, then turned on the water. She couldn't get her clothes off fast enough. They smelled like sweat, blood, and that odd combination of plastic and sanitizer produced by hospitals everywhere.

The smell didn't discourage Frank from using them as a bed while she showered.

CHAPTER 30

Shannon didn't leave the shower until the cold water forced her out.

She grabbed one of the white towels hanging on the back of the door, dried herself off, and slipped into her room where she got dressed to the first couple tracks on Kurt Vile's album, *B'lieve I'm Goin' Down*.

His music always got her thinking clearer.

Soon as she slipped an old Cubs T-shirt on, hunger came back at her. Michael had probably wrapped her plate and put it in the fridge—he was always better about saving leftovers than she was.

She left the music going in her room and walked out to the kitchen.

Michael sat at the table with his laptop in front of him. More investigating, probably. If that's all he was getting into, she was better leaving it alone. Why get upset at him for doing a bit of Facebook snooping?

Over his shoulder, she saw some new picture of Isabella, Colm, and Robbie. They were at a nightclub together.

They sat in one of those big, white leather sectionals, like something straight out of Scarface. Jimmy Butler, the Bulls' best player, sat next to them—on Colm's left. An open bottle of Dom Perignon was on ice in front of them. "Colm wasn't shy about bringing his money problems on himself, was he?" She reached into the fridge and grabbed out her saran-wrapped plate.

"No, he wasn't." Michael's fingers were interlaced in front of his mouth.

She popped the plate in the microwave.

"Don't microwave fish." He whipped around in his chair. "You'll ruin it, and you'll make the entire building stink. Eat it cold."

Shannon scrunched her nose at the idea. "I'd rather eat my own foot."

She started the microwave.

"Keep that attitude up, and I might arrange it," Michael said.

She looked in his direction to sneer, but when she had a second look at his computer screen, she froze.

"What?" Michael looked at his computer. He looked back to her. "What is it?"

Shannon moved closer to his laptop. Maybe her eyes were playing tricks on her and she hadn't seen what she'd just thought she saw.

"Did Colm ever think Isabella cheated on him?" She stared at the picture.

"He never really talked about it," Michael said. "But I'm sure a girl who looks like her had plenty of chances if she wanted to."

"I think she was," Shannon said.

"What? Why?"

She pointed at the bottom of the picture. It was barely noticeable, obscured by all the bright lights flashing in the club and a few glasses sitting on the table in front of them. Jimmy Butler clear on the other side of the photo probably grabbed everyone's attention, too. You had to use your imagination to see it, because it was half-buried by Robbie and Isabella's legs, but it was there.

Robbie's fingers interlaced with Isabella's. The two of them held hands. They looked happy with each other.

CHAPTER 31

The security guard out front of Mitchell Hospital was the same guy Shannon had flipped in the hallway on her way out of Isabella's room earlier this evening. He wasn't pleased to see her.

"I don't care who you work for," he said, already waving her off as she approached the front door of the hospital. "CPD, FBI, NRA, NAACP—turn around right now and get off my campus. I ain't got the patience for you."

Shannon could barely make eye contact with him. She was deeply ashamed of what she'd done to the poor guy. She held her hands up, careful not to spill any of the coffee she'd bought.

"I've come to make peace." She held a coffee out for him. "I was wrong. I want to apologize for tweaking your arm earlier—"

"Tweaking my arm?" he said. "Lady, you flipped my ass onto the hospital floor!"

"And that was wrong of me to do. I know you were only doing your job, and I should've listened when you guys told me to stop."

"You're damn right you should have." He took the coffee. "I ain't paid enough to fight a cop."

"Very few people are." Shannon took a sip from her own coffee.

"Ain't it late for you to be drinking that?" the guard asked.

"I think I've got a long night ahead of me."

"Oh, yeah? What you working on?" He took a drink from the cup she gave him.

"When you saw me today, I was after a girl," Shannon said. "I think she has a part to play in a murder case."

He looked at Shannon like she was crazy. "Why didn't you say nothing before?"

"I was busy."

He laughed.

"If I had said something, would that have made any difference?"

"It damn-well might have," he said.

"Right. I'm sure you all would've put your tasers down as soon as I screamed I was on a case."

"I ain't saying you wouldn't have gotten shocked once or twice." He sipped the coffee. "But it wouldn't have gone further than that, that you have my word on."

How nice.

"Is that a professional courtesy or a hint of chivalry?"

"All of us here got respect for the work you folks at CPD do," he said. "Male or female."

"Does that mean you'll let me visit the girl I'm here to see?"

He considered that for a moment. Then, as if he thought better of it, he grabbed the radio on his shoulder anyway. "What's her name?"

"Isabella Arroz."

The guard let go of his radio. He didn't seem too pleased to hear Shannon request to see Isabella.

"Had to be her," he said.

"What?"

"Your girl left today."

"That was quick," Shannon said.

"Damn quick. So quick she forgot to make arrangements for her baby's body."

A chill washed over Shannon. "She left the baby behind?"

He nodded. "I been doing this job twenty years, and I ain't never seen anybody leave their own kid behind like that." He looked up at the moon like it had some kind of answer for him. "I mean, we understand grief and all that, sure, but ain't once have I seen a mother leave her child like that girl Isabella did."

How was that possible? Isabella had been so drugged when Shannon had seen her a couple hours ago, she'd had no idea who Shannon was. How could she have left the hospital? And what mother would leave behind her baby's body?

"Did anyone see her go?"

"The front desk, probably, but they all swear they didn't," he said. "The way all those ladies get talking with each other, it's a miracle they spot anybody coming or going through that door. Anyhow, we got her leaving on camera."

"She wasn't alone, was she?" Shannon asked.

The guard shook his head. "You want to see the video?"

"Not if she left with a guy missing half his ear."

The guard looked surprised at Shannon's guess. "How'd you know that?"

"That's her brother," she said. She turned around and started through the semicircular drop-off and pick-up zone in front of the hospital.

"Goodbye!" the guard called after her. "Nice talking to you."

There was no time for any of that. She jogged through a flower bed out front of the hospital and didn't stop until she was at the front passenger door of Dedrick's car.

"What'd he say?" Dedrick sat behind the wheel, looking nearly as beat-down as Shannon, but somehow still fresh. She was lucky he didn't have the kids tonight, or she might've not been able to convince him to come along.

"He said we need to go check Isabella's house." She buckled her seatbelt and closed the door.

"All right," he said, "but did you have to give him my coffee?"

"Coffee is a better social lubricant than alcohol. I had to get him talking."

Dedrick put the car in drive, then hunched over the wheel and sighed. "You keep treating me like this, and one of these days, I'm gonna leave you," he said.

CHAPTER 32

From down the street, Dedrick and Shannon didn't see any lights on in Isabella Arroz's home.

"You think they're actually asleep?" Dedrick asked as he turned the car's engine off. They parked near the corner—just far enough to keep out of sight of anyone who wasn't looking for them.

"If they're in there, not a chance," Shannon said. "You ready?"

"I am if our boys are."

Shannon put her short-range radio to her mouth. "Check in."

Six other officers answered her call. They'd stationed themselves at various points around the Arroz household. Two waited in their cars—one in front of the house, and one in the alleyway behind—in case someone tried to run. Two more officers would join Dedrick and Shannon at the front door, and the final pair of officers would take the back door.

Everyone was ready to go.

"Looks like our boys are punctual tonight," Dedrick said.

Good. Shannon was concerned that the short notice of her request would equate to holdups, but everything fell into place.

"They're not all 'boys.' You should use a more gender-neutral term." Shannon pulled back the slide on her Glock. "It's a new millennium."

"Sure," he said. "Does that mean we're hitting the showers together back at the station?" Dedrick flashed a cheesy grin at her. He popped the trunk, then got out of the car before she punched him in the leg.

"What an enlightened attitude." Shannon joined him at the rear of the Impala.

He picked through papers, binders, and all sorts of mundane things needed for their jobs. He kept it all in his trunk. Along with a hard shotgun case.

Dedrick pulled the case forward. He sat it on top of a grocery bag which held a spare change of clothes, should they ever have to work in bad weather.

The case's latches clacked open under his thumbs. Inside, his black Remington 870P laid on gray egg-crate foam. There were two boxes of shells next to it—one filled with triple-aught buckshot, and the other with rubber slugs.

He slid the shotgun's pump forward then slipped in six rounds of buckshot.

Shannon was content with her Glock. That's all she'd ever needed.

"Ready when you are," Shannon said.

Dedrick pumped the shotgun, chambering a round. He jammed another shell into the receiver. "Let's do it."

"Move in," Shannon said into the radio.

She and Dedrick started down the street, hunched over like they were in a war zone. They crouched behind trashcans, leaned up against fences, hid behind a car which had been left at the curb for so long that the city had paved the latest coat of asphalt around it.

All the while, Shannon kept an eye on Isabella's house.

Nothing had changed. No lights came on, no blue glow from a TV radiating through the curtains in the front window—not even a porch light from the old man's half of the duplex next door.

They met the pair of officers assigned to breach the front door with them at the end of Isabella's driveway. Shannon saw the second pair of officers—the team assigned to the house's back door—hop the fence into the backyard.

Good so far.

"Go!" Shannon whispered.

She, Dedrick, and the pair of officers with them sprinted for the front door.

On the porch, one of the officers brought his battering ram to bear on the doorknob.

Dedrick went first, shotgun aimed into the house. "CPD!" he yelled.

Shannon followed, yelling, "Police! Get on the ground! Police!"

The two officers at the back door yelled similarly. "CPD! Get down! On the ground! CPD!"

It all mixed into an unintelligible flurry of screaming, anger, and spittle in the darkness. Lights flipped on in the house. Children cried and screamed from the back.

No one in the living room.

The officers in the rear of the house signaled to Shannon that the kitchen was also clear.

Shannon caught Dedrick's eye. They paired off and went to clear the bedrooms together.

They moved down the small hallway. Was that someone's footsteps? She couldn't hear it over the sound of children wailing. Was that a gun being cocked? They stopped at a door decorated with stickers of Mickey Mouse and his pals, the Ninja Turtles and Daniel Tiger.

Dedrick busted the door in with the butt of his shotgun. "CPD!"

"Police!" Shannon yelled as she came in behind him. "Police! Get down!"

The children screamed bloody murder.

Shannon turned the lights on. As soon as the room lit up, Dedrick swung his shotgun down fast as he could.

Isabella's little brother and sister sat huddling each other, tears streaming down their faces, mouths twisted in horror. They were balled up with each other on a twin bed made up with sheets from the new *Star Wars* movie.

Shannon checked the closet, to make sure someone wasn't waiting to ambush them. Nothing in there but a smattering of clothes, shoes, and an old comforter bag filled with toys. She holstered her Glock and turned her attention to the kids. They were in hysterics.

"It's okay, guys." Dedrick tried to calm them down by running his fingers through their nests of dark hair. "We're here to help you—we wouldn't hurt you. We're the good guys."

The sobs slowed down. Dedrick knelt at the side of the bed, his big hands on each child's shoulder.

"I'm sorry for scaring you guys," he said. "We wanted to help you. We thought there might be bad people in here."

"What?" The little girl began crying harder. "Bad people?"

"No, no, sweetheart, don't cry! They're not here."
Dedrick stroked her cheek. "Don't worry. Detective
Rourke and I just checked—no bad people anywhere in
here, right?"

"Right," Shannon said. "I just made sure, personally."
One of the officers leaned into the room from the
hallway. "House is clear. Nobody home."

"See?" Shannon said. "No bad people."

Both children looked relieved by this. The little girl
wiped tears away with her hands, and the little boy
brought the sleeve of his Ninja Turtles pajamas up under
his nose to wipe away his snot.

"We're safe?" the girl asked.

"Of course!" Dedrick said. "I wouldn't let any bad
people make you guys unsafe. I'm a police officer."

The little girl cracked an unsure smile at him.

Dedrick took a spot next to them on the bed. His leg
smothered Kylo Ren's face on the bedsheet. "Can you
guys tell us something?"

Using a glance, the kids checked with each other.

"Did Isabella come home earlier?"

"I don't know," the girl said.

It wasn't hard to see she wasn't telling the whole truth,
so Dedrick turned to the little boy, who couldn't have
been older than seven. "What about you?"

"Bella said if you guys come here, we aren't supposed
to—" The little boy slapped both hands over his mouth.

"Stupid!" The girl pushed him. She was probably
somewhere around ten.

"Hey, now," Dedrick said. "Be nice to your brother.
He's not stupid. He just wants to tell the truth. That's a
good thing." He looked at the boy. "Right?"

The boy nodded. His hands stayed over his mouth.
"But Bella told us not to talk to you," the girl said.
"She said police are bad guys. She said you'd arrest us and beat us up if we talked to you."

"Did she say that?" Dedrick said. "We're talking now, aren't we?"

"Yes." The little girl didn't sound too sure of that.

"Have I arrested you?"

She shook her head. The little girl had the same shining, straight, black hair as Isabella, and it swayed across her shoulders.

"Have I beat you or your brother up?"

She checked with her brother, who shrugged. "I guess not."

"Well, what do you think then? Am I a bad guy?"

The little girl studied Dedrick for a moment. She narrowed her eyes, as if she could peer through any lies he might have veiled himself in. She looked him up, down, and all over until she was satisfied that maybe, just maybe, this time, her older sister had been wrong about this one thing.

"How about you?" Dedrick said to the boy.

He dropped his hands from his mouth, threw his head back, and laughed.

"Does Detective Rourke look like a bad guy?"

"She's a girl," the little girl said back. "She's not a guy!"

"That's true." Dedrick beamed at her. "So, if I'm not a bad guy, and Detective Rourke *can't* be a bad guy, what does that make us?"

Both kids pondered this for a moment. It was a thoughtful question to consider. What answer would this police officer with the friendly smile and the tired eyes want them to say? What would get them in trouble, and what wouldn't? And how could they rectify their answer with what Isabella had told them already?

They'd have to navigate carefully.

"Good guys!" the boy said.

"That's right!" Dedrick said. He held up his hand for a high-five, and the little boy slapped his palm.

Shannon couldn't help but smile. Even given the circumstances for why they were here, who wouldn't think that was cute?

"So do you guys think you can tell us the truth now?" Dedrick asked. "Do you know where Isabella went?"

Again, the kids looked at each other. They conversed with their eyes quite a bit, these two.

"Yes," the girl said. "She and Afonso went to Canada."

The hair on the back of Shannon's neck stood on end. If Isabella and Afonso made it to the border before the authorities were alerted, they were good as gone. If they didn't, and Border Patrol picked them up, things would be a lot harder all around.

She started to say something to Dedrick, but he held up a hand while keeping his eyes locked on the kids.

"Okay," Dedrick said evenly. "Canada. Can you tell me how you know Isabella and Afonso went there?"

The girl looked around the room. Her hands chased after each other in her lap. However she came by that information, she didn't want to say it out loud.

"It's all right," Dedrick said. "You won't get in trouble. I promise."

Her mouth twisted into a grimace. "I was up past bedtime. I like to play in the closet sometimes."

"That one?" Shannon pointed to the little closet in the corner of the room with the bag of toys inside.

"Yes," the girl said. "Sometimes I hear Bella and Afonso talking."

Shannon walked over to the closet. She pushed the clothes on hangers aside, then pulled out the plastic comforter bag with all the toys.

"Through the wall?" Dedrick asked.

The little girl shook her head. "I heard their voices."

Shannon took the shoe boxes off the shelf at the top of the closet and sat them on the floor. Short as she was, she couldn't quite see if she'd cleared the shelf or if there was anything else on it. She shined her light up there and saw the very top edge of a metallic vent cover shine back.

"A vent," she said. "In the closet."

"That wall is shared with the living room," Dedrick said. "I bet that vent goes straight through."

He turned his attention back to the little girl.

"This is very important, okay?" He looked straight into her eyes so she could see he meant business. "Even if you weren't telling the truth before about anything you said, you have to now. I promise I won't get mad if you lied."

"Okay." She nodded.

Dedrick grabbed her little hands. "You're sure your sister said the word, 'Canada?'"

"Yes." She pointed to a map of North America pinned on the stretch of wall to the right of the bedroom door. "Canada."

"Can you go over to that map and point to Canada?" Dedrick said.

She hopped up from the bed, and reached up toward the map. Her finger touched Canada—exactly on the stretch of land which connected to Michigan over the St. Clair River.

"Do you know where they went?" Dedrick said. "What city?"

"No."

"I do," Shannon said.

CHAPTER 33

edrick and one of the officers stayed behind with Isabella's little brother and sister.

The rest of the team who'd stormed Isabella Arroz's home followed behind Shannon as she raced to I-94 with the lights and sirens blaring from Dedrick's Impala.

"Dispatch, this is 411," Shannon said into the radio.

"Go ahead, 411."

"I'm in pursuit of a black Chrysler 300 with a cracked rear windshield," she said. "I believe the vehicle is eastbound on I-94, possibly heading for Windsor, Canada."

At the time, Shannon hadn't realized what Isabella meant when she'd uttered the word "Windsor" in her hospital bed. Now it all made sense. Windsor, Canada. That's where she and Robbie—not Colm—had decided to flee after Robbie took Ewan's eighty thousand dollars from Colm and killed him in an effort to frame Ewan.

Windsor, Canada was where Isabella and Robbie planned to start their new lives with their baby.

"Understood, 411," the dispatcher said. "Do you have a description of the driver of your vehicle?"

"Possibly Arroz, Afonso, or Arroz, Isabella," she said. "They're brother and sister, they're likely together, and they should be considered armed and dangerous. They're wanted for conspiracy to murder."

"Copy, 411," the dispatcher said. "We'll get all the help we can out there."

That's all she could ask for.

Shannon swerved around a minivan too slow to pull off to I-94's shoulder and laid on her horn. Were lights and sirens from four separate CPD cars not enough to get these people to move the hell out of the way?

God only knew how big of a head start Isabella and Afonso had on them. They could be well into Indiana by now. Hopefully, they hadn't gone that far. The toll roads should slow them down, even at ten o'clock at night—that was, assuming Afonso didn't have an I-Pass on his car, allowing him to go through the toll without stopping.

She hoped they wouldn't be stupid enough to try the border. By the time they got there—if they got there—Homeland Security would smother them, and Isabella's arrest would be largely out of Shannon's hands.

Maybe she could talk them out of it.

Shannon held tight to the wheel with her left hand and grabbed her cell phone with her right. She swiped the screen with her thumb. Her eyes darted between the road ahead and the phone's screen. She navigated to her recent call list, then dialed Isabella's number.

After one ring, she answered it.

"Hello?"

"Isabella?" Shannon didn't wait for Isabella to say anything back—she could hardly believe her call had been answered at all. "I know you're running to Windsor. You have to stop your car. Pull over to the side of the road and toss your keys. CPD will be there shortly. I can help you, but I can't do anything if you make this harder than it has to be."

She waited for Isabella to respond, to tell her to go to hell, to say anything at all, but all Shannon heard was a sniffle and the sound of wind rushing around a car's cabin.

"Isabella, please," Shannon said. "I know about Robbie. I know he helped Colm rob Ewan. I know you and Afonso were part of the plan to murder Colm—pull the car over and I'll come get you."

The line disconnected.

Shannon slammed the phone against the seat out of frustration. This wasn't going to end well if the two of them insisted on running.

She turned the phone over and slid her thumb across it so hard and fast, she was surprised the screen didn't shatter in her hand. She called Isabella again.

It went straight to voicemail. She called again. *Come on, Isabella, don't be stupid.*

Voicemail.

"Dammit!" Shannon shoved the phone back in her pocket.

She stomped on the gas pedal, passing a line of trucks pulled off to the right shoulder. At least they knew what to do when the cops came buzzing up from behind.

"411, I think I've got your suspects," someone's voice cracked over the radio.

Shannon scrambled for the mic. "Go ahead."

"I'm near mile marker 34," he said. "I'm looking at a black 300, with a crack clear across the rear windshield. Plates are registered to Manuela Arroz. Probably a relative of your suspects."

Probably. "Okay," Shannon said into the radio. "Have they seen you?"

"Don't think so."

"Then hang back," she said. "If they haven't started running yet, don't let them catch wind of you."

"Well, I'd love to," the officer said, "but there's a whole mess of CPD cars coming up behind me with their lights on and sirens going."

Who the hell would that be?

Shannon craned her neck, trying to get a better view of the road ahead. That's when she noticed the tiny green sign at the side of the road. Mile 34.

"That's us," Shannon said into the radio. "We're coming in support."

She pushed the gas pedal all the way down to the floor. The Impala lurched forward. The tachometer climbed upward, ever closer to the redline.

A gout of dust shot up from ahead.

"He just crossed the lane!" someone shouted over the radio. "He's going into incoming traffic."

Shannon watched Afonso's car skid across the grass between the east and westbound lanes of I-94. He reached the westbound lane and spun out. Shreds of rubber leapt off one of the rear tires of his car as it fishtailed off the far side of the road.

The car went backwards off the north shoulder of I-94, down a hill covered in overgrown grass and whatever garbage people threw out of their windows on the way to Chicago.

If only Shannon had her Jeep handy. She crossed over I-94 westbound, a tad more in control of her vehicle than Afonso had been, praying that Dedrick's Impala wouldn't get totaled in the process. In her rear-view mirror, she saw the other CPD cars following behind her and to her side. She saw the interceptor who'd first spotted Afonso's car go screaming across a stretch of road to the east.

Shannon hit the far shoulder and went down the hill. She lost sight of everyone in a mess of kicked-up dirt, grass, and weeds that probably hadn't been mowed since last year—if not longer. She did her best to keep the Impala in the tracks left by Afonso's 300, hoping that if there were any debris, he would've picked it up ahead of her.

She heard a loud *thunk*. The wheel of Dedrick's car shuddered. Hopefully, she hadn't just run over Afonso or Isabella.

But before she had a chance to look behind her, the grass subsided, and a large building appeared before her.

Afonso left his car parked in the building's shadow. It looked almost like an aircraft hangar, except for the large, seized conveyor belt jutting into the air from its side.

The doors and trunk to Afonso's 300 hung open. Each tire was worn down to the rim. The car's hazard lights blinked. Probably an automatic response to all four tires being shredded to nothing. She doubted Afonso cared much about anyone's safety.

She stepped on the brake pedal and the Impala skidded to a stop in a mix of weeds and gravel. Shannon took just enough time to slam the car's shifter into park. She nearly leapt out of her car, her hand already reaching for the Glock on her hip.

"Out of the car!" she screamed. Though she didn't expect to see Afonso or Isabella emerge from it.

Neither one did.

She buried her eyes behind the sights of her weapon and approached the car slowly. If anyone came skittering out with bad intentions, she fully planned on pulling the trigger. Shannon wouldn't miss.

Behind her, a few of the other CPD cars skidded and stopped at the bottom of the hill.

A couple steps off the bumper of Afonso's car, she flung the trunk's lid up. Nobody inside. Nothing except all the things she'd seen when Isabella showed her Colm's bag at the station this morning.

Could one of them have hid in the back seat? She opened the rear door.

Two booster seats for children. That was it.

No one in the front of the car either.

"Where they at?"

Shannon looked over her shoulder and recognized Officer Coughlin—the safe-smasher from Colm's house.

"Let's hope they aren't in there." She nodded toward the large, abandoned building. "If they've decided to set themselves up inside, we're in for a long night."

"They armed?" Coughlin asked.

"I take it you didn't get a chance to look over Afonso's record," she said.

"I was a little busy on the way in," Coughlin said. "My reading and driving ain't what it used to be."

"He's armed," she said. "I'm sure of it."

A couple more officers gathered around Afonso's abandoned car.

"So, what's our play then, Detective?" Coughlin asked.

"We need to secure the buildings," she said. "If any of you have a shotgun, or if you've taken assault weapons training, now's the time to break 'em out."

Coughlin grinned.

CHAPTER 34

"Eight of us here now," Shannon said, "and three buildings to secure. I put a call into dispatch for backup, and I'd rather wait for more people to show up, but I don't think we can afford to. If Isabella or Afonso take off for that tree line to the north, we'll have a hell of a time finding them, so we need to get on it. Partner up with somebody. If you have a shotgun, make sure you partner with somebody with a Glock."

The officers began talking amongst themselves, dividing into pairs.

"Woulda been nice if one you mooks did assault weapons training," Coughlin said. He smiled at Shannon. "I got an 870, you got a Glock. What do you say, Detective?"

She nodded at him. There was a psychotic sort of charm to him—not that she looked at him in *that* way. He was probably good with a shotgun.

"Is everyone paired up?"

She was met with nods.

"Good. Here's the plan: Officer Coughlin and I will take this largest building to our west." She pointed at the big conveyor building. "I want you two to take the smaller north building." She tapped an officer by the name of Ross—she didn't see his partner's name. "You two take the east building." She pointed at Officers Wright and Edders. "It looks like some kind of admin building, so I'm guessing there are lots of offices. Take your time. When Coughlin and I clear the largest building, we'll help you sweep that one out."

"You two," she pointed at the last pair—Officers Raab and Knowles. "I want you walking that tree line to the north. It's up to you to find any signs that our suspects have taken off. If you see *anything*, radio me immediately. I'll be available through Coughlin's com. Anyone have a question about their assignment?"

No one said anything.

"Let's go."

CHAPTER 35

"They're in here," Coughlin said quietly. "I can smell it." He stepped over a rusted car axel, bent at the middle.

The possibility existed. He and Shannon entered the building through the south door, which was unlocked and hanging open. Afonso and Isabella couldn't have had more than half a minute to escape his car.

Something rattled across the floor. Shannon whipped around and pointed her Glock at it. A possum's beady eyes glowed green in the light from her flashlight.

"Little bastards," Coughlin said. "Place is probably crawling with them."

There were plenty of places for rodents to hide. From the look of it, whoever owned this scrap yard used this building as housing for large items waiting to be demolished—some washers, dryers, and refrigerators—but mostly cars. Deformed hunks of sheet metal and rubber were stacked five-high in some places. The towers of cars looked unstable enough that if someone were to lean too hard against them, they'd be caught in an avalanche of rusted steel.

"You think our perps might be hanging out above us?" Coughlin scanned the catwalks overhead with his eyes. "I know if I were waiting to ambush somebody in a place like this, that's where I'd be."

"If they're smart, they won't be waiting in ambush," Shannon said. "They'll have already taken off for that tree line."

"Yeah, well, every gang banger or criminal I ever met in this city was pretty much a dumbass," Coughlin said. "Judging by that little bit of stunt driving back there, I doubt these two are breaking the streak tonight."

A door creaked open somewhere beyond a wall of cars ahead of them.

"Did you hear another unit pull up since we've been in here?" Shannon said.

Coughlin grimaced at her and shrugged. "Hey!" he yelled. "You guys CPD over there?"

No one answered

"What the hell was that?" Shannon hissed. "If our suspects are in here, you just made us both a target."

Coughlin shrugged. "Like you said, they probably ain't—"

A gunshot cracked through the warehouse.

Coughlin fell backwards into a pile of radiators, screaming.

On reflex, Shannon hit the ground, then grabbed him by the shoulder straps of his body armor. The adrenaline screeching through her veins gave her enough strength to shimmy up to the wall of cars ahead of her in mere seconds, all while dragging Coughlin along.

Another spray of bullets gnawed into the dusty, concrete floor. Sparks kicked out of an engine block hanging halfway off a crane.

"I'm hit!" Coughlin bellowed. "Son of a bitch, I'm hit!"

More shots barked out from the darkness. They were loud enough to split eardrums. The high ceilings and all the hard surfaces made each shot echo into the others. It was impossible to tell exactly where the bullets came from, how many were fired, or even if there was more than one shooter.

"Detective, you gotta help me!" Coughlin yelled.

She grabbed the radio off his shoulder. "Dispatch, I have shots fired and an officer wounded," she said over another burst of gunfire. "I need an EMT immediately!"

"What's your twenty?" dispatch said back.

"We're still in that old scrapyard north of I-94, near mile marker 34."

"We'll get help out there right away. Hold tight."

Another group of bullets hammered into one of the cars Shannon and Coughlin huddled against.

"Where are you hit?"

"It's my leg," Coughlin said. "Got me in the damn thigh."

She turned and looked him over. It was too dark to see anything.

"Don't take this the wrong way." She put her hands on his thighs, feeling around for blood. Once she found it, she felt for a wound. Once she found that, she took Coughlin's hand. "Keep pressure right here," she said.

He did as told, though he groaned and threw his head back. "What a way to end a shift."

"I'm gonna get a tourniquet together," Shannon said. She couldn't see how bad the wound was, but if he'd been hit in the wrong spot, Coughlin could bleed to death in a few minutes.

A pile of car parts laid to her left. She crawled on her belly over to it. She might be able to scrounge up and something to tie around his leg like a windshield fluid line or a piece of weather stripping from a door. She picked through the pile.

More gunshots cracked off, and the bullets hit behind her—she hadn't been spotted.

Then, on the far side of the warehouse—its north end—the sound of a door being kicked in joined the mix.

"CPD! Drop your—"

Whoever it was, they were cut off by more gunshots. Shannon hoped to God someone else hadn't gotten wounded on behalf of her case.

She sorted through the pile a little quicker now. Shannon threw aside old bolts, she pushed a brake drum out of the way, and sent the housing for a rear-view mirror flipping into the dark.

Then she found it. An old seat belt. She couldn't have picked a better tourniquet if she wanted to.

She scrambled back to Coughlin on her elbows and knees.

"How you holding up?" she asked over a cackle of more gunfire.

"Oh, just great," he said. "Never felt better."

She went to work, wrapping the seatbelt around his thigh, above the wound. She grabbed her little flashlight out of her pocket.

"That's good," she said. "Because you're about to feel a lot worse."

STEWART MATTHEWS

She tied a half-knot with the seatbelt, then laid the flashlight against the topside of the half-done knot, then finished tying it around the flashlight.

"Hold onto something," she said. "This is the bad part."

He grabbed the handle of a smashed car door and gritted his teeth.

"Ready?"

Coughlin nodded.

She turned the flashlight like a spigot valve. With each turn, the seatbelt constricted Coughlin's thigh. She continued rotating the flashlight and tightening the belt until it didn't want to give any more slack. For his part, Coughlin weathered it well. She was sure she'd bumped his wound once or twice in the process of tightening the tourniquet, but he never did more than groan from behind his teeth.

"Hold this." She took his hand and put it over the flashlight. "Whatever you do, don't let go."

A fresh round of gunfire popped off.

Shannon grabbed Coughlin under his armpits. She had to get him out of here.

"What the hell are you gonna do?" he asked. "Wish me out of here?"

"I'm pulling you out."

"The hell you are. I got a hundred pounds on you, easy."

She grunted and pushed against the ground, trying to get some leverage on Coughlin by making her legs do the work. It took everything she had to move him two or three inches.

"Told you," he said.

"Shut up."

There had to be something she could do.

Someone grabbed her shoulder. Shannon whipped around.

It was a SWAT officer, ready for a fight. "Where's the shooter?"

Shannon pointed in the general direction of where she thought Afonso or Isabella was—she still wasn't sure who had the gun. "I need to get this man out of here," she said. "He's been shot in the leg."

The SWAT officer waved a couple of his men up. One holding the tourniquet, they picked up Coughlin and slung his arms over their shoulders.

"I knew you weren't taking me out of here," he said to Shannon as they helped him toward the door. "But you get an A for effort."

She smiled and gave him the finger.

A shot whizzed overhead. They all ducked—no one was hit.

The SWAT officer motioned for the rest of his team to follow him. Four men moved up.

"I think the shooter is overhead," Shannon said. "In the catwalks. But I haven't seen a muzzle flash, and there's a crazy echo in here."

"We'll find him," the SWAT officer said.

"Any of your people carrying a carbine?" Shannon asked.

One of them leaned up against the front end of a car. He rested his elbow on the hood, and in his hands, he held an AR-15 assault rifle.

He squeezed off a shot.

She watched the bullet pierce through the darkness overhead like a white-hot needle.

Someone cried out in pain. Afonso.

"Is he dead?" she asked.

No one answered. They all waited for another burst of gunfire. None came.

"Let's go find out," the SWAT officer said.

They took a set of rickety metal stairs up to the catwalks, each officer with his weapon drawn and ready to fire in case someone laid in wait.

The only person they found was Afonso Arroz. He was on his back; the AK47 he used to attack them was halfway off the catwalk. Shannon and the SWAT officers approached him. She kicked his rifle off the catwalk and kept her Glock trained on him.

"He's alive," she said.

His chest rose and flattened. He'd caught the bullet in his pelvis—near his right hip. The bone had likely been obliterated, and he'd passed out from shock, pain, or both.

The SWAT team picked him up and dragged him out.

Once outside the large building, she saw an ambulance waiting. The top of Coughlin's bald head stuck up over the edge of a partially upright stretcher in the ambulance's back. The EMT looked at him, and Coughlin's hand moved as if he were retelling what happened inside the scrap mill just now.

He'd be okay.

"Medic!" the SWAT Officer yelled.

A second EMT came out of the ambulance's cab. He stole a quick glance at Afonso, realized they'd need another ambulance, then picked his radio up and made a call.

"I'll let you take him from here," Shannon said to the SWAT officer. "Thanks for having my back in there."

"No problem." He whipped off a little two-finger salute.

Shannon made her way toward Coughlin. She had to talk to him, if nothing else but to double-check that he was actually as unharmed as he looked.

But something else grabbed her attention—a flicker of light moving over by the tree line about a hundred yards off. A white spark in the darkness.

A cell phone screen.

Shannon's phone vibrated in her pocket. She pulled it out.

Isabella was calling her.

CHAPTER 36

"Tell me he's alive." On the other end of the call, Isabella sounded as if she were the emotional equivalent of broken glass. "Tell me you didn't kill my brother."

Shannon looked toward the spot against the tree line where she'd seen the pinprick of light. It was gone, but Isabella couldn't be far.

"He shot at us first."

"So you *murdered* him?" she yelled into the phone. A rage pushed at her voice unlike anything Shannon had heard—and she'd heard some rather unhappy people during her stint with the Corps, though most of them hadn't spoken English.

"I know you can see us," Shannon said. "Why don't you come back here and we'll talk about Afonso? If you want, we'll talk about how you put Colm up to taking that money from his father. And we'll talk about how you convinced Robbie to murder for you. We'll talk about everything, even the baby."

She heard Isabella intake a sharp breath.

"I know what it's like to lose a baby," Shannon said. "Let me help you, Isabella."

There was a long pause until Isabella said, "Goodbye."

Shannon put her phone back in her pocket and ran toward the tree line. She knew it was stupid not to tell at least one of the dozens of uniformed officers nearby. She knew it was a tactical mistake to go up against someone whom she knew had probably spotted her. She should've turned around, waved down the SWAT team, and gone home to cuddle up next to Frank.

But she didn't have any other choice. If anyone else was around, she couldn't be honest with Isabella. She'd lose her nerve if anyone else was there to hear her talk about her miscarriage.

She'd go home to Frank tonight and cry. She'd cry for a week straight, all in private. She'd have to wrestle with her demons all over again, and she'd feel that much worse knowing that she'd left someone else to do the same.

It was a mistake, yes—but a mistake that had to be made. Shannon wouldn't be able to live with herself otherwise.

The grass whipped at her knees as she ran. Little stones tried to twist her ankles, and fireflies buzzed past her ears.

"Isabella!" Shannon yelled, though she couldn't see her. "Isabella, come talk to me!"

There was another flash in the darkness. It wasn't the sharp glow of a cell phone screen. It was a burst of heat, light, and hatred.

A bullet whizzed past Shannon's head.

She flopped to the deck as fast as she could. What kind of moron wouldn't have thought Isabella was armed? Shannon could've slapped herself for being so hasty.

"Isabella!" She'd only lifted her face far enough off the ground to yell. "I know what you've been through today. Please, I'm begging you—let me help you. There's a way out of this, but you have to stop running."

Shannon laid in the dirt for a few seconds, hoping Isabella would give herself up. She heard her heart pound in her ears. The crickets played to the summer moon. Her fellow officers scrambled in the distance behind her. They must've heard the shot, but she doubted anyone saw it.

No response from Isabella.

From some deep corner of her brain, AJ's voice admonished her for bringing birdshot to Iraq. She didn't have a clue what she'd gotten herself into.

Over the tops of the trees, she heard a helicopter engine push closer. Time was running out. As soon as the chopper flew overhead, it'd spot Isabella, and the arrest would be made before Shannon could talk to her.

Shannon pushed herself up to her feet.

This job made everybody a little crazy. Clearly, Isabella wasn't in the mood for a heart-to-heart, but Shannon was.

She slowed up and walked toward the tree line, which was about ten paces off. The grass thinned out. The toes of her shoes bumped into gnarled roots, and a raccoon scurried away from her.

She didn't have the slightest clue where to go. Isabella could have doubled back and lost her when she dove to the ground. For all she knew, she'd have the muzzle of a pistol pressed into her back at any moment.

A chainlink fence rattled ahead. It was close.

"Isabella?" Shannon pressed herself up against a tree. She wouldn't catch a bullet this time. "I know it sounds like a lie—like I just want you to give yourself up—but I can help you. Not just with your part in Colm's murder, but with what happened after."

The fence rattled again. She heard Isabella grunt in frustration.

"I saw you in the hospital today," Shannon said. "I know you're scared about the baby being premature—you're worried about what happens next, but there are people who can help you."

"I can't take care of that baby," Isabella said. "I can't."

Shannon decided to risk it. Unsure if she'd get her head blown off or not, she peered around the tree. It took her a second to pick out Isabella's shadow against all the trees and bushes, but she spotted her.

She was trying to squeeze through a hole in the fence, a bag in one hand and a pistol in the other. The bag was caught on one of the open chain links.

"Is the money in that bag?" Shannon asked.

For a second, Isabella's eyes met Shannon's. And the next second, the muzzle of her pistol looked big enough to swallow Shannon whole.

The gun belched fire. It happened three or four times in quick succession.

Splinters flew out of the tree Shannon covered herself with. The first splash of them hit Shannon's shoulder. They whipped her with a lash of pain—absent one second, and there—full-force—the next. It knocked her off her feet and she screamed through clamped teeth.

She'd been sprayed by mace during her academy training. She'd been shot by a .38 once in the vest when helping deal with a parole violator. She'd had a blast from an IED knock her unconscious in Iraq while flipping her truck and subsequently snapping her leg.

But none of it had felt like this.

When she brought her hand up to her left shoulder out of reflex, the pain worsened. Shannon's entire body cramped up in agony. Ends of splinters stuck out of the shoulder of her CPD T-shirt in the pale moonlight. It was like she'd sprouted quills.

Shannon got up to her feet. She leaned against the tree on her good shoulder. For a moment, she considered pulling some of the larger splinters out, but thought better of it. Someone else could deal with that later—but not her, not now.

Her left arm hung off her body, totally useless.

The helicopter buzzed overhead. They wouldn't be able to spot Shannon or Isabella under the trees.

With her right hand, she grabbed her Glock from its holster. She wasn't sure what she was going to do with it—there was no scenario in which Shannon would be able to bring herself to shoot Isabella—but holding her weapon made her feel safer.

She peeked around the tree again. The hole in the fence was empty.

Being a bit shorter than Isabella, Shannon didn't have as much trouble negotiating her body through the gap. She got all the way up to her bad shoulder without a hitch. Then she knocked a few splinters against the fence and bit back a howl.

She carefully brought the rest of herself through the fence. She wiped sweat off her brow with the back of her forearm. When she did, something on the ground caught her eye.

Shannon bent down and picked it up. It was a crinkled twenty-dollar bill.

An entire trail of them laid before her.

She followed it.

Some of the bills in the roots of trees, some stuck in the low-lying brush, and others rolled in the slight breeze.

That's what Isabella struggled with. She couldn't get herself and the bag of Ewan's money through the fence at the same time. She'd ripped the bag open and left behind a trail that would lead Shannon straight to her.

"Isabella, I'm here," Shannon said. Hopefully she was in earshot. "I know you made a mistake. Everyone makes mistakes—I've made mistakes."

The trail of money thickened. Shannon kicked a pile of it hiding behind a thicket of weeds. She stopped and looked at her feet. She must've been standing in over ten thousand dollars in small bills.

"Running away isn't going to solve anything," Shannon said. "You have to work through your problems. You have to become a better person because of them. You have a baby back at the hospital depending on you to be a good mother."

The CPD helicopter roared as it swooped past. Its spotlights briefly shined through the trees. Shannon saw she was at the edge of a creek. Like dead leaves, dollar bills drifted with the current.

About ten paces away, Isabella sat with her head in her hands and cried at the edge of the water.

The bag was at her side, deflated. She'd lost all her money.

Shannon kept her Glock lowered.

"I can't raise that baby." Isabella must have noticed her standing there. "I can't do it—I'm not strong enough."

"I know you can," Shannon said. "You're stronger than you think."

Isabella laughed bitterly. "I wasn't strong enough to handle Colm. I had to bully my brother and Robbie into doing it for me." She rubbed her arm across her eyes. "How can I take care of a baby that small?"

Shannon couldn't answer her. She didn't know the first thing about caring for a child.

"Do you remember talking to me in the hospital?" Shannon asked.

"I don't want to remember anything about the hospital." Isabella picked her head up and planted her hands in the mud behind her with her legs sprawled out before her. One of her arms gave way, and she crashed into the muck.

Shannon wanted to reach for her.

Isabella laughed. She lifted her face out of the filth and cackled. "The nurses said my coordination would be bad. But I had to get away."

"I know you believe that, but running isn't going to solve anything," Shannon said. "I know."

"Yeah? You know so much. I'm sure you know what it's like to see a two-pound baby come out of you. You know how it feels when the nurses roll your baby away in a plastic box because it can't breathe on its own. You know the dread that comes with knowing you're responsible for that baby on your own because his father threw his own life away."

"I'm not claiming I know what that's like," Shannon said.

"And you don't know how to help me either," Isabella said. "Did you know I called Robbie? I begged him to stay away from Ewan, but he said as long as Ewan was alive, the Irish would keep sending people after Afonso."

"I answered his phone when you called," Shannon said, remembering the Pizza Hut number. "I'm sorry about what happened to him, but running from your child isn't going to solve anything."

"Running is all I have left," she said. "I made Afonso sneak me out of the hospital. I didn't want that baby with me. But I guess that plan is done—neither of us thought I'd lose all the money in the woods." She laughed and wiped a handful of mud off her shirt.

"Where's your gun?" Shannon said. "Did you lose that in the woods, too?"

"No."

Shannon's Glock came up straight away. The sights lined up with Isabella's forehead.

"I'll save you the trouble." Isabella brought her revolver up.

"Drop it!" Shannon screamed. The hair on the back of her neck stood on end. Her finger struggled to grasp the trigger. She couldn't shoot Isabella. "Put it down!"

"You'll be fine."

Isabella pressed the gun to her temple. Its barrel reflected the spotlights from the helicopter as it made another pass overhead, and Isabella's over-sized, watery eyes threw back the red and blue lights dancing so far away.

Her finger wrapped around the trigger.

The gun's action came at Shannon in slow motion. The hammer reared back. The cylinder turned to drop a fresh round behind the gun's barrel. The gun clicked, as the hammer reached the apex of its backward motion.

It started forward.

CHAPTER 37

Shannon kept her eyes open, unable to do anything. She watched Isabella's face as the revolver's hammer gobbled up millimeter after millimeter of space between it and the round's primer.

Isabella wore a relaxed—almost bored—expression as she waited for the hammer to slam down on the primer and fire the bullet. Strands of her black hair caught the light, summer breeze and wrapped around her neck, around her wrist, and around the barrel of the gun.

The hammer clicked. It struck the bullet's primer to no effect. By some miracle, the chambered round didn't fire.

Isabella's hand went limp. The gun fell into the mud.

Shannon ran to the revolver. She scooped the gun off the ground. She holstered her Glock while she held the revolver at her left hip—as high as her injured shoulder would let her hand go. She pulled the cylinder out. Nothing but empty casings dropped into the mud at her feet.

Shannon's knees turned to putty. She sank to the ground. "Why would you do that?" she screamed.

Isabella had no answer. She cried. She looked like she'd just walked away from a plane crash.

Shannon wrapped her one good arm around her. Isabella shuddered, even recoiled for a moment, but then she gave in. She sank into Shannon, and the tears poured out from both of them.

"I came here to help you," Shannon said.

"No one can help me." Isabella's entire body strained. It took her full effort to get the words out. She wheezed and sighed. "I'm broken."

"You're not broken."

"I abandoned my baby—what kind of mother does that?"

Shannon let her go. She looked Isabella in the eyes. She remembered being that confused and heart-broken once. It felt like the entire world had tumbled out of control around her, and nothing could make it stop.

"I miscarried once," Shannon said.

Isabella shook her head.

"It's true. It happened in Iraq," Shannon said. "There was a guy—a corporal in the Second Marines who I'd run into a couple times at Camp Lejeune. We had a fling—a couple dates, a night at the Marine Corps ball, but we were both shipped out before anything more happened.

"Then I saw him over there. We crossed paths near Ramadi. I'd been assigned there for a couple weeks to run supplies, and his battalion passed through. It was one night. That's all. Nothing more than that." The tears stung Shannon's eyes. "A while later, there was an IED."

The words stuck in her throat. It had been years since she'd told this story. Isabella was the first person who'd heard it outside of Shannon's support group.

"I didn't know I was pregnant until after I woke up in a hospital in Germany, and the nurse looked at me. She was horrified. She asked me why I didn't tell anyone I was pregnant. I lost my only baby, and it was my fault," Shannon said. "I couldn't let you do the same thing—I couldn't let you run away."

CHAPTER 38

A week after arresting Isabella and Afonso Arroz at the Smitwick's Metal Recycling Yard, Shannon walked up to the big front desk at the Logan Correctional Center.

"I'm here to see Isabella Arroz." Shannon held up her star for the desk officer. The name "Felton" was stitched into the dark-blue patch over the right breast pocket of her shirt.

Ms. Felton didn't appear impressed by Shannon's star.

"Did you schedule an appointment?" She didn't look up from her copy of *People* magazine.

"I called yesterday," Shannon said. "I asked for two p.m. I know I'm a little late."

Ms. Felton broke her eyes away from an article about the anniversary of Ben Affleck and Jennifer Garner's divorce just to glare at Shannon for a moment. "It's 3:30."

"I know I'm late," Shannon said. "But, please, would it be possible to do me this one favor?"

Ms. Felton grabbed the handset off the stone-gray phone next to her. As she dialed, her finger stabbed the number pad in a silent protest against Shannon's perpetuation of injustice.

"I've got a visitor for Arroz," she said into the phone.

A pause. The person on the other end of the line said something barely audible to Shannon.

"The new girl," Ms. Felton said. "The pretty one. She came in yesterday."

Another pause.

What would Shannon say to Isabella? *Hi, sorry I arrested you, did you know your baby passed before you left the hospital?* She hadn't even had a miscarriage. What kind of advice would Shannon give her?

She sighed.

No advice. She'd have to listen. She'd have to be patient and listen to Isabella tell her whatever it was Isabella wanted to tell her. If she wanted to talk about how gross the showers were, okay. If she wanted to lament the lack of beauty supplies, good. If she wanted to complain about the food, fine. Shannon was ready to spend the entire afternoon listening to someone tell her how wrong it was that nearly everything at Logan CC came pre-packaged.

But then, maybe Isabella shouldn't have conspired to kill Colm. Maybe she shouldn't have fired on Shannon.

Her shoulder throbbed.

She couldn't bring that here. She didn't come to blame Isabella, or to judge her for things she'd done. How could she possibly listen to her if she was too busy resenting her?

This was Shannon's healing process, too.

"She doesn't want to see you," Ms. Felton said.

"What?" Shannon said. "Are you sure you talked to Isabella Arroz?"

"Yes."

"Did she say why?"

"It's not my job to know, Detective."

"Can't you make her come out?"

"We have regulations and codes to follow, too, ma'am. For instance," she stood up from behind her big desk and pointed at Shannon's feet, "that blue line you're standing on is to be crossed by staff *only*."

Shannon rolled her eyes. She took half a step back, stamping the heels of her cross-trainers against the gray linoleum for emphasis.

"What about a police officer who's come to speak with an inmate?" she said. "What're the rules on that?"

"Is your visit part of an official investigation?"

"Oh, come on," Shannon said. "It's a prison. *Make* her come out."

Ms. Felton forced a polite smile. "At Logan *Correctional Center*, we believe—"

"Fine," Shannon snapped. She turned and walked toward the glass double doors at the front of the lobby. She opened one partway and stopped. "If you're *allowed* to," Shannon said, "tell Isabella I'm coming back. Tell her I'm stubborn, and I'll wear her down long before I'm worn down. Tell her she can't run from me forever."

Shannon showed herself out the door before Ms. Felton said anything back to her.

Outside, Dedrick leaned on the hood of his Impala and thumbed through his phone. Frank lay about five feet away, up against the building's facade where it was nice and shady.

As soon as he noticed Shannon, he hopped up and came running for her.

"How'd he do?" she said to Dedrick.

Dedrick reached out and patted Frank on his hip. "He was great. We took a quick walk, but the whole time, he kept looking at those front doors. I think he wanted to make sure he'd be here the second you came out, so I brought him back."

"Sounds like my guy." She smiled at Frank and scratched him under his collar. He leaned into her. "I appreciate you meeting me here. I wasn't sure how I'd feel when I came out of there, and ... well ... you're—"

She looked at Dedrick's pretty brown eyes and whatever she was going to say flew from her mind.

Way to keep it together, Shannon.

"I'm just glad you came," she said.

"Me too." He smiled at her for a moment before his eyes darted down to his phone.

"Anything interesting?"

"Actually, yeah," he said. "I got a call from a friend at DCFS. They placed Isabella's little brother and sister with a great aunt of theirs. From the court documents she sent me," he held his phone up, "it looks like the aunt had tried to contact Isabella and Afonso a number of times over the past four years, but they kept dodging her."

"Why would they do that?"

"I had the same question," he said. "People like Isabella and Afonso like to scam the system by keeping checks and food stamps meant to help with the kids. At least that's what my girl over there said."

"Your girl over there?"

"You jealous?" Dedrick's face lit up with a smile.

She blushed.

Dedrick floated up from sitting on the bumper of his car. He had a look in his eyes. One that Shannon knew meant trouble, but she couldn't help being drawn to it. She'd seen that look in her mind, at the moment when the two of them dropped all the veils of friendship and professionalism between them. The moment when they finally owned the feelings they tried to keep hidden from each other.

"I noticed you'd packed your Jeep," he said softly. He was close enough that the smell of his cologne wrapped her in cedar. "I thought you might have, but I wish you hadn't."

Her heart beat so fast and hard, she barely heard him.

"There was something I wanted to give you before you left for good—something I've been thinking about for a long time."

He brushed his fingers across the back of her hand.

Completely unbidden, Shannon closed her eyes. His arm reached around the small of her back, and all conscious thought melted from her. He pressed her body against his. The muscles in his chest practically enveloped her, and she loved it.

Shannon wanted nothing more than to lay her ear against him and listen to him breathe, listen to his heart beat, and to hear the sound of his voice resonate in him as he confessed to her all the things she ached to hear.

His other hand came up from her shoulder blades. He cupped the back of her neck. Her heart rapped against the inside of her chest in anticipation. She almost couldn't stand it anymore.

Mercifully, Dedrick brought his lips to hers. They were gentle as butterfly wings. His hand slid into her hair, his fingers weaved through her loose curls, and finally, the two of them locked to each other.

She pressed into his kiss. Shannon wanted to explore every part of his lips—the small creases, the soft skin, the way they made her weak when he smiled.

With Dedrick holding her, she was small and she was vulnerable—but she was safe. Nothing could reach her here. Nothing from her past could torment her. Nothing would pull them apart, if that's what they both wanted.

She pushed herself away.

"Dedrick—" Shannon looked up and into his soft eyes.

"What's wrong?" He let her slide out of his arms.

Why had she ruined that moment? Why couldn't she let something beautiful *be* beautiful without destroying it with her own hang-ups? She could have cried.

"I'm sorry," he said. "That was stupid of me." He handed her Frank's leash, grabbed his keys out of his pocket, then walked toward the driver's door of his Impala.

"Wait," she said.

He stopped.

"It wasn't *that* stupid," Shannon said.

Dedrick smiled at her, though he couldn't totally wash the disappointment off his face. "When you make it to Stockholm," he said, "forget about me."

Her heart could have shattered right then and there. Why did she let her insecurities get in the way of everything good in her life?

He got in the car and started the engine.

Frank barked once at him. Shannon waved goodbye. Dedrick tapped the horn and drove off.

She wanted to tell him her Jeep wasn't packed for Stockholm. With the mandatory time-off for physical therapy for her shoulder, she'd finally got her chance to take Frank to the Indiana Dunes.

After that, Shannon would be back in Chicago. She'd be back on the job for CPD.

CHAPTER 39

"I got a hundred on this one." Miss Honey slapped a hundred-dollar bill on the top rail of the pool table. "You up for it?"

Michael watched the guy she played against look back at his friend resting an elbow on a nearby table and sipping a vodka tonic. He shrugged.

"You won three outta four so far, bro," he said. "She wanna lose a hundred, that's her problem."

His friend had taken Miss Honey's bait, but her opponent still looked unsure.

"Come on, sugar," she said, "gimme a chance to win something back."

He rubbed chalk on the end of his cue stick. "Rack 'em up."

"There we go!" She clapped. She walked over to the coin receiver, placed her quarters in the slide, and pressed it in. The balls rolled out like thunder in the pool hall.

She wasn't losing this game.

"Another cranberry juice?" The waitress put her hand on the crook of Michael's elbow.

"Sure," he said. "And get her another whiskey sour." The waitress looked at Miss Honey. "The lady at the pool table?"

"Yep."

"You two aren't, like…." She looked at Michael across her eyes. "You know."

"We're not," he said.

The waitress smiled at him. "Okay, then, I'll be back with your drinks."

Back at the pool table, Miss Honey hooted after sinking two balls on the break. That guy she played had no idea what he'd just been roped into. Nobody around here did. That's why they'd driven all the way out to Kokomo.

Michael's phone buzzed in his pocket. He took it out and looked at it. A number he didn't have saved in his contacts was calling him. Normally, he wouldn't answer, but he wanted to step outside for a smoke anyhow. He tapped the green answer button on his phone's screen.

"Give me a second," he said into it.

The music in the pool hall was too loud to carry a conversation, so he stepped through the side exit just past his table.

Once out in the muggy, Indiana air, he trapped the phone between his shoulder and his ear. "Go ahead," he said as he dug for his father's cigarette case in his pocket.

"Michael?" It was a man's voice—dry, but smooth.

"Who is this?"

"It's Ewan."

His skin turned clammy. He stopped fishing for the cigarette case. "How'd you get this number?"

"I heard through the grapevine that someone claiming to work on my behalf went looking into my son's murder."

"Oh, yeah?" Michael said. "That was nice of someone."

"I know it wasn't you," Ewan said. "You're smart enough to stay out of something when the bosses ask you to."

"That's right." Michael grabbed the cigarette case and flipped it open with his thumb.

"Still, it's peculiar that someone sneaking around, looking into Colm's death, would say they worked for me. Most people wouldn't care for all the trouble that may come with telling a lie like that. Most people wouldn't care to investigate my son's death at all."

Michael lit his cigarette. "Yeah, most people in Chicago tend to their own business—or so I hear."

"Most people," Ewan said. "But someone who was close to Colm might lack good sense."

"No argument from me." Michael puffed his cigarette. The line stayed silent, until he thought he heard the sound of ice clinking in a glass. A car drove past, blasting Kendrick Lamar over the stereo.

No one spoke. It was as if he and Ewan were feeling each other out through the dead air, judging intents, making future plans and counter-plans. Until finally....

"Goodbye, Michael," Ewan said.

The call disconnected.

Michael finished his cigarette, then went back inside to see how Miss Honey's hustle went. He knew he'd only be able to ignore Ewan Keane for so many years.

DETECTIVE
SHANNON ROURKE
SERIES

SIGN UP TO MY MAILING LIST AND GET CHICAGO BROKEN

Chicago Broken - *Detective Shannon Rourke Book 2* (normally $3.99) for 99 cents on release day

I'll also email you a couple times a month what I'm working on, what I'm reading, and other books I think you should try.

WEBSITE
http://www.StewWrites.com/

FACEBOOK
https://www.facebook.com/StewartMatthewsAuthor/

EMAIL
stew@stewwrites.com

ACKNOWLEDGMENTS

My deepest thanks goes to my wife, Arianna, for putting up with all the nights I locked myself in my office and pecked away at this book, and all the others, published and unpublished.

Thanks to the Honorable Salvador Vazquez of the Lake County Superior Court Criminal Division for lending his legal expertise as it pertains to warrants and the legality of investigative tactics.

And thank you to all my friends and colleagues at the Author's Corner, notably Mike Omer and Shayne Rutherford for their beta reads of Chicago Blood and for being my sounding board, and Perry Constantine for his keen eyes.

Made in the USA
Coppell, TX
26 April 2023

16079293R00164